The
Chronicles
of
Doodah

The
Chronicles
of
Doodah

George Lee Walker

HOUGHTON MIFFLIN COMPANY

BOSTON

1985

Library of Congress Cataloging in Publication Data

Walker, George Lee.
The chronicles of Doodah.

I. Title.
PS3573.A4253324C5   1985   813'.54   85-5220
ISBN 0-395-38174-6
ISBN 0-395-40726-5 (pbk.)

Printed in the United States of America

For Edith
Wife, Friend, Believer

The
Chronicles
of
Doodah

1

AT FIRST, I don't want to talk about the fear to anybody. It's just another layer on top of those that already exist, all the fears that most company people have — fear of the boss, fear of making mistakes, fear of embarrassment, fear of losing your job, fear of not getting promoted like everyone wants to be. All of those are definable fears, not as bad as the nameless fear that you worry about the most. Has anyone coined a word for it? It's the fear of the Company itself, as if the Company were some kind of monster, something alive.

Where this fear comes from, I don't know. And I don't know if anyone else has it, because people never talk about their fears. Where fear is concerned, everybody takes the Fifth. Talking about fear could be self-incriminating.

My idea is that a lot of this vague fear comes with the territory. It spreads like smoke through the corridors, up the elevator shafts, and right into all the offices. People smell it, breathe it. Sometimes it gets so thick it causes their eyes to water. But nobody ever mentions it, because that could cause a lot of trouble.

Headquarters are the worst, and I work in headquarters. My theory is that a lot of the fear comes out of the building itself, like some kind of dangerous emission from plastic. This may sound crazy, but it's not so crazy if you think about it. If you walk through an old, deserted house with cobwebs and creaky doors, you're scared. Maybe corporate headquarters doesn't have cobwebs and squeaky doors, but it's just as frightening as a haunted house in some ways.

For one thing, you're all alone. Oh, sure, there are other people around, but you know they won't help you if there's trouble — a mass murderer hiding in a closet, a flock of rabid bats ready to pounce, or a floor about to collapse and send you plummeting to your death.

The real source of this unnamed fear has a lot to do with the surroundings. Like a haunted house, a corporate headquarters isn't the most habitable place in the world. It's a huge, lonely place designed to show the world how rich and powerful the Company is. It doesn't have things that are the least bit tacky, like gumball machines. It is clean, polished, and very quiet.

Our headquarters sits in the middle of a huge tract of vacant land in a suburb of a large, decaying city. From a distance, it is just a large chunk of onyx, and you can't even tell that it has windows until you get up close. When you are driving to work in the morning and you see this looming monolith in the distance, growing larger and larger, you feel like an explorer in the desert, slowly approaching a towering butte.

There aren't many sidewalks around our building, just one in fact, a kind of concrete catwalk that keeps you from falling onto the acres of carefully groomed grass. Conrad and I like to walk around the building on this solitary sidewalk after lunch. Except for the people working on the lawn, we never see a soul.

"You'd think they would put a bench or two along this sidewalk," Conrad always remarks on these walks. But there is not a bench to be seen, and nobody has the nerve to sit on the grass. The grounds are not meant for people.

Inside the building there's that peculiar corporate silence. You walk to the elevator in the morning and stand in a group of people who look vaguely familiar, like people who go to your favorite drugstore. A few of them speak in very low voices, but most of them don't say anything.

They don't say much on the elevator, either. All you hear is the rush of air through the shaft. Once in a while you will hear a muted conversation, but you can't make out the subject. Something about an inventory or a committee report. You never know who they're talking about, either. Everything is "he" said this or "they" will act on that soon. You can ride up and down on the same elevator with the same people, year after year, and never get to know them. They are from other departments and get on and off at different floors. They may have power over you or they may not. The chances are they do.

Maybe the silence of the headquarters breeds some of the fear I was talking about. Laughter and loud voices are never heard. Most of the time, all I can hear in my office is a steady hum. I don't know exactly where it comes from. But sometimes it is louder than at other times, and sometimes it clicks off altogether.

Maybe silence creates fear. I suppose studies have been done on this. Maybe it's not the silence itself but the unexpected noise that disrupts the usual quiet.

Like the time we heard the voices of children in the corridor.

Gloria, my secretary, came rushing in.

"Sir! Sir!" she said in a loud whisper. "There are children out there!"

I calmed her down as well as I could. It was the first time we had ever heard children's voices on our floor. We learned later that they belonged to the children of a new secretary, come to see where their mother worked. The secretary was spoken to, and it never happened again.

Yes, silence may create some of the fear. But having nothing to do probably creates a lot more.

I'm not a psychologist, but I do think guilt is probably behind a lot of this fear. They pay you a high salary, and a lot of the time you are just sitting there, the top of your desk clean and only that mysterious corporate hum to remind you that you're still alive.

At any moment, the boss could pop into your office and find you doing nothing. In fact, this has happened to me several times, and the odd thing is that he doesn't seem to care at all. Maybe he spends a lot of time doing nothing, too.

Maybe having something to do is not at all important. Maybe the boss doesn't care so long as you continue to be part of his head count. He wants his head count to be larger than so-and-so's head count. The bosses have armies, and while they rarely have to send them into battle, the size of an army is a very important deterrent against aggression.

Anyway, I sit here at my desk brooding about a new fear. It's a fear I really don't need, on top of my fear of Marlott, my boss, and of getting fired, or not promoted, or of saying something in a meeting that is just ignored.

This fear is worse than all the others. It keeps me awake nights, keeps me from thinking about my work, causes palpitations, nausea, sweaty palms. This new fear is driving me crazy.

Things keep happening that have no place in this quiet, ordered environment. Strange things that anyone else would call illusions or hallucinations.

Whatever they are — visions, sightings, whatever you want to call them — I have been walking down a dark passageway of fear and panic ever since the first of these events.

Let me say right now that on the surface, anyway, these incidents don't appear to be particularly threatening, things like the dog or the pigeons. So far, nobody has come at me with an ax, and I haven't yet found a bomb under the hood of my car.

Maybe it would be better if I had, because events like that are almost normal during high crime times like these.

No, these incidents just don't fit in. They are the kind of things that never happen in a corporation, things that I could never mention to anyone except my good friend Conrad. And I haven't told even Conrad about all of my sightings. I'm very tempted, but I know he would think I am crazy.

Conrad does know about the dog.

It happened just after I came back to my office after a meeting with Marlott. I was feeling pretty good because Marlott liked my draft of a speech. I couldn't figure out why my door was closed because I always leave it open. Gloria, who hadn't been at her desk, couldn't tell me.

I opened the door and walked in to find a huge dog sitting in my chair. It was a German shepherd.

At first I thought it might be a guard dog — trained to kill — although I had never seen one around the building. But the dog just sat there panting and grinning, apparently very happy to see me after a long wait.

For a minute or two I stood close to the wall opposite the desk, warily eyeing the dog and waiting for something to happen. But the dog just went on acting as if we had been friends for years. Cautiously, I made my way over to the chair, reached out, and gently stroked its head.

"There, there, nice dog," I said. The dog got more excited, its body quivering and twitching. It licked my hand and whimpered ecstatically, a very friendly dog.

What should I do? The most sensible thing would have been to call Security and ask them to remove the dog. But Security would ask questions. The incident might even require a written report, with several drafts, meetings, and memos. Perhaps the dog was Conrad's idea of a joke. But Conrad was not one to play practical jokes, especially on me. Maybe the dog had just wandered into the building. But how did he get past the security guards? How did he get on the elevator and how did it happen that he got off on this floor? And, most mysterious of all, how did he end up sitting at my desk with the door closed?

I pushed Conrad's key on the intercom.

"What do you want?" he growled. He had been in a lousy mood lately.

"There's a dog in my chair," I said, laughing for the first time.

"Look, I'm working on something right now," Conrad shouted. "I've got no time to play."

"I'm not playing. There's really a dog in my chair. Come and see for yourself."

"I can't come over and I can't talk. Marlott's on my ass. I've got to get this thing finished."

"I'll be over," I said.

Why I decided to go see Conrad is beyond me, but I didn't know what else to do. Conrad didn't look up when I walked in. He kept typing furiously, the muscles of his face so strained that I hardly recognized him.

"I'm not kidding," I said. "Come on over. Take a look. A dog. Come on, it'll only take a minute."

"Christ!" Conrad exploded, jumping from his chair. He rushed past me into the hall. "Anything to make you happy."

My door was closed, although I could swear that I had left it open in the excitement.

"Go on. Open it. See for yourself."

Conrad cautiously opened the door and walked in. He turned around abruptly and stormed out, almost knocking me down.

"Shit, I'm gonna lose my job," he screamed. "Quit wasting my time with these stories about dogs sitting at your desk!"

I walked into the office. The chair was empty. I went over to the desk. The chair was pushed in as far as it would go. That is the way I always leave it. That is the way I left it when I was called into Marlott's office to get his reaction to my speech. I examined the papers on my desk, but I found all of them where I had left them. The dog had simply disappeared. There was no sign that he had ever been there.

2

I TRY TO PUT THE DOG out of my mind, but it doesn't work. One reason it doesn't work is that other things keep happening. After a nighttime trip to Marlott's house, I begin to feel that I am really losing my grip.

We are all afraid of Marlott anyway. There is something about him, something you can't put your finger on. On the surface, he appears to be harmless — a man in his early sixties, a big, pipe-smoking Frenchman who talks about fishing all the time. That is, he talks about fishing whenever he talks, which isn't often.

But something is lurking behind the friendly fisherman act. Conrad and I are baffled by it and we talk about it endlessly. What are we afraid of? All we can point to is a kind of nameless menace, almost a murderous quality, that you can see in his eyes.

The story is that he studied for the priesthood but left the seminary under a cloud. He has been with the Company for something like forty years. Part of his success, they say, dates back to the Company's earliest years, when he was supposed to have performed some valuable service for the Founder. Some say he even saved the Founder's life.

Sometimes Marlott has Conrad and me drop off speech drafts at his house. He is in a hurry, he says, and needs to read them as soon as they come from our typewriters.

There is an odd thing about these speech drops, and Conrad and I have talked about it a couple of times. No matter how often we make one of these drops, we arrive to find no one at home — the house all dark, the curtains drawn, and no cars in the driveway.

Marlott lives in a far suburb, on a street where the lots are at least an acre. There are no street lights, and I always have a hard time finding where he lives.

One night I drove along the gravel road he lives on, looking for his house. To my surprise, I didn't have much trouble finding it, because the porch light was on, the number was clearly visible, there were lights inside, and there was even a car in the driveway.

I rang the doorbell and waited. I rang again, then a third time. Then I banged the big, brass knocker against the mock-colonial door. I must have stood there for five minutes. Nothing.

I peered through a small crack between the drapes. I had trouble deciphering the scene, but I could make out Marlott, his big fisherman's body slumped into an easy chair, peering up at one of those giant television screens that more and more people think they have to have.

A short, dark man stood next to the screen, watching, a pointer in his hand. I couldn't make out what they were watching, but it seemed to be some kind of meeting, people sitting around a table. Their faces were too small for me to recognize.

Suddenly the action on the screen stopped. The man with the pointer reached over and pushed a button on a controller. A giant face appeared on the screen, and this time I had no trouble recognizing it. It was my own face.

The man raised the pointer to the screen and began touching it to my features. First my eyes, then my mouth. He was talking, looking first at the screen and then at Marlott. Marlott appeared just to sit there, nodding from time to time. My face remained on the screen for a minute or so, then the action of the meeting resumed.

The next time the action stopped, the screen showed a picture of the whole group. Again, I tried to make out the people, but their images were too small. The short, dark man was pointing at one of the people at the table who appeared to be writing something. The man said something, Marlott nodded in agreement, and the videotape started moving again.

I watched this scene for about ten minutes, trying to figure it out. I tried the bell again and banged the knocker. They must have heard me, but no one came to the door. So I left the draft behind the storm door, got into my car, and drove back to the office.

I worried a lot about that incident but came to no conclusions. It wasn't exactly life-threatening, but it made me very nervous. Was the man a psychologist or personnel expert who was critiquing my performance in meetings? Very possibly, but why was all of this going on behind my back? Maybe they were thinking of promoting me. Maybe they were thinking of firing me.

The scene at Marlott's house was just one of those corporate mysteries you worry about. What really panicked me was my trip up to the thirty-second floor to pick up some material from the Chairman's office.

I rode the elevator to the thirty-second floor, the highest

in the building except for the penthouse. This was the pinnacle of power, the goal of a thousand ambitious men, as tough to conquer as the summit of Everest. It was a lonely redoubt of stark and cold splendor: marble walls and deep blue carpeting that absorbed what little sound there was. Only twenty men had their offices on this floor; they were the lone survivors among the thousands who had spent their lives scheming, smiling, acting, and working, working, working for a chance to share these privileges. The lucky twenty had their own elevator, which no one else could use on penalty of dismissal, and their own masseur, a dour Swede with bulging muscles and a T-shirt printed with the Company's logo. There was even a vice-presidential shoeshine boy, a small, light-skinned black named Sam who always wore an outrageously large straw hat. I had shared an elevator once with Sam. He smiled constantly and muttered little pleasantries like the blacks in Shirley Temple movies. There was even a vice-presidential gym with, I was told, beautiful female attendants. And of course there was the vice-presidential dining room, where these barons could order anything they wanted with the reasonable certainty it would be available. Every vice president had two secretaries and an executive assistant. The secretaries were on this floor, but the assistants had offices below.

Above this floor was the penthouse, a complex of living quarters so isolated that its existence was only conjecture. Only a few men claimed to have ever seen it; the rest of us had to be content with second- or third-hand reports. The living quarters were the exclusive province of the Chairman, but he rarely used them, favoring instead one of the eleven houses he owned around the world. Still, we were told that the Chairman sometimes stayed overnight in the complex with one of his several mistresses. Again, this point was a matter of speculation. It was true that certain high-ranking executives would catch a rare glimpse of the Chairman on his way to his office. But he, too, had a special elevator, which not even the vice presidents could ride. Since security was especially tight in this part of the building, and since the Chairman seemed to come and go when people were already in their offices or had long since gone home, no one ever saw him in his special elevator with his mistress of the day. In any event, the Chairman's limousine was parked in a remote spot shielded from view in the underground executive garage. The Chairman could step out of the limousine into his elevator and ride up to his living quarters without being seen by anyone. Of course, he could stop at his office. But if he chose to go on to the living quarters for a midmorning snack or cocktail, he could be certain of prompt and meticulous service, because the living quarters were staffed around the clock by a crew of maids, cooks, and assistants, all of them eager to do his bidding.

What little we knew of these arrangements we learned from one or two vice presidents who were willing to talk to us about such things with cautious glances and hushed voices.

I thought of all this as I made my way along the thick carpeting to a centrally located reception area, furnished with sofas in white and blue leather and with the works of Joan Miró, Picasso, Rauschenberg, and other moderns on the walls.

At the center of this reception area was a large semicircular desk, behind which sat two men. The identity of these men changed from time to time, but they all looked very much the same — big, burly men in their sixties with the hands of wrestlers or prizefighters. These men were reputed to have spent their early years with the Company in the plant security forces. In fact, one of them had been spotted in an old newspaper photograph of a famous battle between company goons and plant workers attempting to organize a union.

Then in his twenties, he could be seen in the photograph beating a union man over the head with a club. Now, on certain days of the week, he sat behind the large desk, looking like a grandfather at a wedding in his dark, three-piece pinstripes.

The brawny ex-goons were supposed to be receptionists, and they performed their duties with notable courtesy and charm. But there was something exaggerated about their solicitude; we guessed they were here primarily to protect the floor's occupants. Other companies might well have employed uniformed security guards for this purpose, but our Company is especially sensitive to appearances. After all, who would want to harm our top executives, whose dedication to the public, generosity, and overall decency were widely recognized? In reality, the desk that the men occupied was a guardpost in corporate dress, a guardpost equipped with the most sophisticated security devices.

When I arrived at the desk that afternoon, the men on duty were studying the television monitors that sat on a shelf just above their knees, hidden from outside view. I walked up to the desk and waited to be recognized.

"Yes?"

"I'm here to pick up something from the Chairman's office."

"Do you have an appointment, sir?"

"Not really. I don't need one because I'm just going to get something from one of his secretaries."

"What's your name and department, sir?"

When I gave him the information, the guard smiled and said politely, "Would you mind waiting over there?"

I sank into one of the couches. A large clock with brass hands and little squares for the hours hummed faintly against the wall above my head.

Bored, I picked up one of the business magazines on the

glass table in front of me. Deadly stuff — trends, charts, numbers, political and economic predictions. I put it down after leafing through the pages and sat thinking about my "sightings."

My reverie was interrupted by a loud flapping sound. Terror overcame me as a fat pigeon swooped down and landed on the floor a few inches from my left foot. Turning abruptly, I caught a glimpse of the guards. They were acting as if nothing were happening, staring stupidly at their television monitors. Just as I started to say something, two other pigeons flew up from the center of the semicircular desk, from a spot right behind the guards' backs, and swooped by inches from my face. The pigeons skittered madly about the room, coming closer and closer each time they passed me. I opened my mouth to shout something, but no sound emerged. I had always been terrified of birds; being trapped in the same room with one flying around paralyzed me. I thought of the time when I was four and a flock of blue jays attacked my brother and me as we walked through an oak grove. I could still feel the beaks of those jays pecking at our heads and hands as we tried to fight them off. My heart was about to explode, and my hands were sweating as I sat frozen in terror, waiting for the attack to stop. Then, to my amazement, the birds flew by in a final salute, more slowly than before, and in perfect, single-file formation, disappeared behind the desk at exactly the spot where they had started their flight.

The guards continued studying the television monitors, their faces blank. A telephone chimed gently; a guard picked it up and spoke softly into it for a second or two before hanging up.

I tried to regain my composure. I took out a handkerchief and wiped my face and hands. Then I combed my hair — a stupid gesture, I later thought.

"That was quite a trick!" I said to the guards. "But

frankly, I didn't think it was very funny. I have a kind of phobia about being trapped in a room with birds."

"Birds? What birds?" one of the guards asked in what appeared to be genuine amazement.

"You know what birds. The pigeons that just performed a little stunt flying a minute ago." My voice was trembling with anger.

"Did you see any pigeons, Carl?" the older of the guards asked.

"No, of course not," Carl replied. "Perhaps you were dreaming, sir."

"Look," I said, "I'm not feeling very good right now. I'll drop by later to pick up that report from the Chairman's office."

The guards didn't answer. When I got up somewhat shakily and headed back toward the elevator, they were still staring at the TV monitors as if nothing had happened.

3

"GET UP HERE right away. The Chairman wants to see us about the first draft of the suppliers speech."

It is Stover's raspy voice. Stover is a vice president, the head of our department, and Marlott's boss.

I throw my draft and notes into a folder and hurry out the door. We are scrambling, so to speak — down the runway and off, up to fifty thousand feet to engage the enemy. The enemy is "them" — Stover and the Chairman — all of them, in fact, who have offices on the higher floors. Push the elevator button and hope for quick action. Adrenaline flows. Stover doesn't like to be kept waiting. The Chairman doesn't like to be kept waiting. No one of their extraordinary importance likes to wait — even for the very few minutes it takes underlings to appear from a few floors below. We know how irritated they are by their behavior when we arrive. Even if the time between their summons and our appearance is only a minute or two, we arrive to find them crackling with annoyance. They are waiting, desks clean, ready to deal with yet another in a constant stream of bothersome subordinates. "What took you so long?" their faces ask. Hurry up. Sit down. Let's get this over with.

So it is when I arrive in Stover's office. He jumps out of his chair and motions me out. We hurry down the corridor, heads down, wholly preoccupied with the coming ordeal.

"You have your copy of the draft?" he asks tensely.

"Yes, of course."

We ride up the elevator in silence. We pass the guards at their station, and this time they hardly look up. They know I am clear to pass because I am accompanied by a vice president. We enter the sacred doors of the Chairman's office. Stover suddenly smiles broadly. He approaches the Chairman's principal secretary, a woman in her sixties, as if she is a movie star.

"Hi there, beautiful. Is the boss in?"

"You can go right in, Mr. Stover." Her face takes no notice of his charm.

Through the walnut doors and into the holy of holies. And there, behind the enormous desk that seems so far away, sits the Chairman, the exalted ruler of a fifty-billion-dollar-a-year worldwide empire with two hundred and twenty thousand subjects.

The Chairman smiles, gets up, and walks to the conference table. I am surprised to see him pull a handkerchief from the pocket of his suit jacket and blow his nose. Stover motions to the chair I am to sit in, and he takes one opposite me.

The Chairman, heavyset and balding, glides into his chair at the head of the long table, sighing with the weight of his responsibilities. Carefully, he arranges his copy of the speech draft on the table before him so that the edges are parallel with the edges of the table. He takes out his glasses, puts them on, then takes them off to polish them with the same handkerchief he used to blow his nose. When he is finally ready, he turns over the title page and begins reading the first page of the draft.

He is a slow reader. I can visualize what he is reading, for by this time I know it by heart:

"I'm delighted to be here and to have this opportunity to share my thoughts with you, our loyal suppliers. It has been a good year for the Company and for you as well, and I want to thank you for the enormous contribution you have made to our success."

I read along on my copy. Perhaps I should have written "chance" instead of "opportunity." But "opportunity" sounded more like the Chairman. "Chance" would certainly have been changed to "opportunity," anyway, by someone along the line.

The Chairman looks up and stares straight ahead at the opposite wall. It is the look of a minister about to begin his sermon on a sunny morning in June, a look of contentment with himself and with the universe.

"Why don't we say 'chance' instead of 'opportunity'?" he asks.

"That's an excellent change," Stover says, tossing me a grim look. "It's more informal, and, after all, you want to strike a friendly tone with these suppliers."

The Chairman reads further, his brow furrowing. Is he having trouble with this speech? Perhaps he is dyslexic. Certainly there is nothing controversial on the first page. Just a collection of civilities, taken from the authorized list.

But the Chairman is still frowning, as if he can't understand what has been written. I glance at Stover, who is fidgeting nervously with a pencil. His eyes meet mine, and the look he gives me is brutal.

The Chairman stops reading. He is staring at the wall

again. Abruptly, he gets up from his chair and walks over to his desk. He stands behind the desk with his hands on the chair and looks out the window with his "This is my father's world" look. Whole hours pass, it seems to me.

"You know," he begins, "what I want to say in this speech is . . ."

Stover motions frantically at me to take notes. He has his tape recorder running, but my notetaking will be a sign to the Chairman that we don't want to miss any part of what he is saying. Perhaps two tape recorders would be even better proof of our devout attention. I make a mental note to bring my tape recorder with me the next time we visit the Chairman.

I scribble furiously as the Chairman gives us his "thoughts." He starts out with the country's trade situation immediately after World War Two. He describes in detail American leadership — economic, scientific, cultural, moral — throughout the world as the war came to an end. He talks about the balance of trade, the factors affecting exchange rates, the supply of raw material, technological transfer, and finally an article he just read on the dynamics of leadership.

"Get a copy of that article," Stover commands me in a voice not so soft that it can't be heard by the Chairman.

"I think it was in the *Harvard Business Review*," the Chairman says. "I'm not sure, but it was one of those top-flight magazines. I'm sure it would be most helpful to you."

"We'll find it, sir," Stover assures him. I know what this will entail. Hours and hours of searching. Many flunkies leafing through page after page of magazines going back several years. And by the time they find something resembling the Chairman's description, the Chairman will have forgotten all about it.

The clock shows the Chairman has been speaking for forty-five minutes. He is now talking about a man he met in Germany a month ago, a noted German economist who sat next to him at some banquet. This man, it seems, had some original ideas about the relationship of Third World mineral deposits to industrial consumption in the West. These were important and original ideas, the Chairman says, ideas that the suppliers would certainly be most interested in hearing. He goes on, talking about inflation levels during the sixties, then turns abruptly to an enthusiastic description of the new front-wheel-drive cars we would introduce two years from now.

By this time, I am almost on the last page of my note pad and my fingers ache from trying to keep up. Stover's tape recorder is still running, fortunately, but if there is something wrong with the machine, which happens occasionally, I will be expected to supply complete and accurate notes on the Chairman's interminable lecture.

I am beginning to get frantic. The Chairman is talking faster and faster, and I am having a difficult time keeping up. His speech is shapeless, without flavor, a gray mass of statistics, anecdotes, old ideas, and banalities, like the utterings of some holy man reciting an endless series of incantations.

Suddenly, the Chairman stops and looks at us. He is very happy, and he smiles. He folds his arms and cocks his head to one side, smiling impishly.

"How am I doing?" he asks.

"Just great — this is terribly helpful," Stover says.

The Chairman is encouraged to go on. But just as he opens his mouth, he looks up at the clock.

"Oh, golly. I've got to be off to the airport," he says. "We'll have to continue this discussion some other time, I guess. I've got some other thoughts — quite a few, in fact."

"Sir, if you would like, my writer here can accompany you to the airport and continue taking down your thoughts," Stover offers. "I just hate to have your thoughts interrupted. What you are saying is very, very valuable to us."

"You know, that's a damned good idea," the Chairman says, beaming at me. "You don't mind, do you?"

"Of course not, sir," I answer. "I appreciate the time you're giving me."

We hurry out of the room, Stover heading back toward his office, the Chairman and I walking toward the Chairman's private elevator.

"As I was saying," the Chairman continues, "the energy crisis of 1973–74 turned the whole industry upside down. We were thrown into a period of reassessment and change that was unprecedented in the history of the industry. We'd been caught with our pants down, I guess you would say, and we had to reverse our entire thinking about the market and try to determine how the dynamics of the marketplace had shifted. The Japanese had become a real force to be reckoned with, and we knew we had to take a good long look at the whole problem of quality."

The Chairman drones on. In the basement garage, his black limousine is waiting for him. His wife, a portly woman with bleached hair, is in the rear seat, smiling at us pleasantly. A waiting flunky opens the doors, and I get in the front seat, next to a burly chauffeur who looks at me suspiciously.

The Chairman continues talking nonstop during all of this, and to show my deep respect for his every word, I continue scribbling away, this time on a new note pad I seized from a secretary's desk on our rush out of the office. The Chairman continues without interruption all the way to the airport. Glancing in the rearview mirror, I can see his wife nodding her approval, smiling in agreement as he moves from one subject to another.

At the Company's hangar, a giant door swings open on our approach, and the chauffeur parks a few feet from the plane, a six-million-dollar jet. The plane's crew is standing by, cheerfully efficient in their pale green uniforms. A functionary opens the door, but the Chairman, in the middle of a "thought," continues talking. He stops abruptly, seized by an idea.

"Say, wait a minute, why don't you come along with us to Los Angeles?" he asks.

"That's a very good idea," I say, happily endorsing a proposal I know is outrageous. Los Angeles is almost two thousand miles away. I have no luggage, not even a toothbrush.

We board the plane, and I get a temporary respite from the Chairman's discourse. The plane's interior is obscenely plush — walnut paneling everywhere, huge easy chairs that swivel around completely, a bar, and a conference table. The Chairman and his wife take seats near the front. I sit down close to the bar near the rear of the plane.

After takeoff, the stewardess serves drinks. My hands, I notice, are cold with rage, and I ask for a double Scotch on the rocks. I toss it off in about three minutes and ask for another. The stewardess gives me a disapproving look but serves it. I settle back to think.

How to get out? How to ease the pain?

Conrad and I often discuss countermeasures. We agree that a kind of psychological lobotomy would be the best relief. If a part of the brain is removed, a certain function becomes impossible. Likewise, if, through a massive exercise of the will, one determines that he will no longer feel the pain of humiliation, then survival becomes possible. We know that this kind of lobotomy works because all around us we see the vacant eyes of those who have operated on themselves successfully.

To the corporation, these people with their expressionless faces, flat voices, sycophantic smiles, and shuffling gait are a source of deep and unending pleasure. These are the good corporate soldiers, front-line troops in the capitalistic wars who will endure any pain to keep their jobs or win a small promotion. The corporation knows that these lobotomites are not destined for high position, because they have clearly lost the spark of ambition. But this, too, is a source of corporate satisfaction. For by giving up the part of their mind that feels, lobotomites remove themselves from the ranks of competitors. The ambitious men are grateful to them for having elected self-destruction instead of competing for advancement. For showing such initiative, and for being cooperative in every way, lobotomites are often rewarded with huge salaries, large offices, and other perquisites. So self-neutralization can have its advantages.

Conrad and I know the dangers, of course. We see men for whom the operation has not been entirely successful. To the untrained eye, they look just the same as others. But to the sensitive observer, they are given away by the smallest of signs, an almost imperceptible tic, a slight raising of the voice in the face of frustration, an ill-timed joke, or even the slightest hint of discontent. Through some slight slip of the knife, these lobotomites have been left with a dollop of feeling. Eventually, their error is sure to come to the attention of the authorities, and they will be given early retirement, transferred to one of the field offices, or, in the rarest of cases, dismissed.

The whole corporate system is designed to humiliate all who receive its benefits. Presidents are humiliated by chairmen of the board. Vice presidents are humiliated by presidents. Directors are humiliated by vice presidents. And so on down the line. Everybody pays, but the price depends on the individual's ability to withstand the humiliation. People with small egos pay the most. The price goes down as the size of the ego increases. In the end, the system strongly favors the egotists and even the egomaniacs. The egomaniacs always believe they are right, and many times they are. Proven right in lesser decisions, they are elevated to positions where they must make big decisions. At the very top, they are free to make choices that cannot be questioned. Their belief in themselves, reinforced by cowed subordinates, huge salaries, and obscenely rich surroundings, eventually becomes a belief in their own infallibility. In the stratosphere they occupy, dissenting voices grow weaker and soon fade away altogether beneath the clouds. They surround themselves with yes men, become addicted to flattery and cant. Some manage to survive this isolation, but they are rare. There are relatively few who last until the normal retirement age. Most of them are forced to leave earlier because of real or imagined mistakes or because they fall victim to "stronger" or "smarter" rivals. But even they leave the corporation with more money than most men ever dream of having.

The most successful corporate people are simply skilled actors who can play well to any audience. To those beneath them, they are contemptuous, cruel, and demanding. To those above, they must appear respectful and devoted. But the greatest danger to people who take up a life of company stagecraft is the danger of overacting. One's humility must not be too apparent to his equals or to his superiors. That is considered gauche, a sign of low intelligence. Likewise, too much honesty can be fatal, and so can too little honesty. Loyalty to one's superiors is never sufficient unless it is complete. One must always agree with one's superiors and speak well of them in the company of others. And of course one must never speak ill of the Company to anyone. All corporate portals should contain the warning, "Abandon free speech, all ye who enter here." This includes the freedom to say anything that might depart from conventional truths about politics, economics, art, literature, or any other subject.

To understand these things as part of the reality of corporate life is only the beginning of wisdom. To endure this reality is the real trick, and many who try it fail. Many of my colleagues have already fallen on the field of battle, victims of alcoholism, drugs, mental disorders, or unacceptable behavior such as a display of anger. One man I knew couldn't take it any longer. He got into an argument with his boss and ended up shouting at him. That man, who has a master's degree in business administration from Harvard, is now a milkman in Little Rock, Arkansas.

We have been in the air only about twenty minutes when I notice that the Chairman's wife has moved across the aisle, leaving the seat next to him vacant. Then I see the Chairman turn around, give me a warm smile, and motion me to join him.

I grab my drink and make my way forward, feeling the effects.

"Where were we?" the Chairman begins as soon as I sit down. "Oh, yes, quality. Well, as you know, I'm sure, we are not talking about real quality, only perceived quality. Japanese cars are really no better than ours, but in fit and finish they look better. It's what's inside that counts, and our studies show that the frequency of repair on major components is much less on our cars than on the Japanese. If we could only get this across to the public, it would make all the difference in the world. That's a big job, but it's one that you fellows in Advertising are just going to have to do and do successfully."

"I'm in Public Relations, Mr. Chairman," I say, surprised at my audacity.

The Chairman's smile disappears for an instant, and his face turns pink.

"Well, no difference. Advertising and PR will have to work together. Now, let's go on with what I was saying about the world car. Time was when automobiles were made in one country and shipped abroad to many different markets. But with inflation and the energy crisis, the whole picture has changed. Now we manufacture parts in many different countries, and the cars are assembled in several countries with only very minor differences in the final product."

Over Iowa, the Chairman is still describing the wonders of the "world car." By the time we pass over Denver, he is talking about the relationship of the yen to other currencies and how the Japanese have arranged to have the yen undervalued so that their products can have a competitive edge throughout the world.

The Chairman's range of interests and breadth of knowledge are impressive enough, but his monologue has the consistency of pudding and the flavor of gruel. I scribble rapidly, writing on the other side of pages I have already completed, hoping that this flood of words might contain some germ of an idea, some thought I might seize upon, as the theme of the suppliers speech.

But somewhere over southern Utah I realize my hopes are in vain. It is not for nothing that Conrad and I have nicknamed the Chairman "the Sponge." His soft, absorbent brain simply soaks up all that he hears and reads — reports, articles, meetings, conferences, dinner conversations, and things his wife tells him. When the time is ripe and he has an audience, his brain contracts and all of these facts and figures, theories and observations, reminiscences and speculations, come oozing out. The ability to distinguish what is useful and important from what is not is beyond him. But this fatal defect seems to be lost on people who know him only slightly or whose contact with him is limited to a brief encounter. In meetings and press conferences, he strikes many people as steady and competent, a serious, solid leader who would not be likely to steer his company into dangerous waters or risk his stockholders' investment with foolish endeavors. What is important is the Chairman's cheerful confidence in the future, his belief in the power of the "free marketplace" to overcome any potential problem.

As the plane approaches the Los Angeles airport, the Chairman turns to me, his face glowing with satisfaction from his long lecture.

"That ought to give you some ideas, eh?"

"Yes, sir. It certainly does. It was an absolutely brilliant presentation of a very complex economic and political situation."

The Chairman is pleased. The plane taxis up to the company terminal and I stand to let the Chairman and his wife disembark. The Chairman's wife turns to me and says:

"I bet you've got plenty of ideas for your speech now, don't you?"

"Yes, ma'am, I sure do. I enjoyed traveling with you, ma'am."

"Thank you, and good luck in your writings."

As the waiting limousine speeds off with the Chairman and his wife, I stand on the warm pavement, gazing at the distant oil tanks through the midday smog, waiting for the pilot and copilot to join me.

"What are the arrangements?" I ask the pilot as he steps down from the plane.

"What do you mean, what are the arrangements?"

"Well, what am I supposed to do?"

"Whatever you want."

"Is anybody picking me up?"

"Not that I know of."

"Well," I say, eyeing a brand-new blue limousine, its engine running, a few feet away. "Can you give me a lift to a hotel? There are some right near here."

"Sorry, we are not allowed to take passengers."

I am incredulous, but there is nothing I can do.

"Well, can you tell me how long you'll be here?" I ask, my voice pleading.

"We'll be returning the day after tomorrow. I'm sorry, but I really don't know what your instructions are."

"I don't have any instructions," I shout, but the pilot and copilot are already getting into the car, ignoring my outburst.

This is ridiculous. All I have with me is what I am wearing and a yellow note pad filled with the Chairman's precious "thoughts." I check my wallet. Twenty-seven dollars. And in my pocket, eighty-five cents. I am marooned in Los Angeles, a vagrant, a corporate Flying Dutchman, doomed to wander forever through this endless, formless city in search of authority.

Was this an accident? I ask myself. Or is it some new device for discarding unwanted employees?

I make my way into the lounge of the company terminal. I head for a phone and call the local corporate field office. Fred Ferris, chief of this small office, comes on the line. I identify myself and tell him what has happened.

"What should I do now?" I ask.

"Gee, I don't know. This kind of thing has never happened before. But don't worry. I'll have a man out right away to pick you up. Just stay put."

Half an hour later, I am speeding along a freeway in a company limousine feeling better about things, beginning to believe that there is nothing at all sinister about my situation. In fact, I'm starting to feel that this is all a lark. I'll get a couple of days out of the office, eat at some good restaurants, and then show up back at my desk with all the nonchalance in the world. And who can question my account of things? The Chairman himself wanted to talk to me, and the best time to do it was on his flight to Los Angeles. How Conrad and I will laugh about all of this! A mere corporate bagatelle, a random, unexpected event in the midst of a perfectly planned, completely controlled routine.

My driver is a cheerful sort, a small blond man with a southern accent, a large diamond ring on his left hand, and very expensive clothes. His bonhomie makes me a bit uneasy, and there is a certain authority to his voice that makes me suspect he may be something more than a chauffeur.

We leave the freeway and drive along a boulevard of expensive shops. Suddenly the driver, whose name is Ron, pulls into a restaurant parking lot. There is a small brass sign by the door: CLUB MAJORCA.

"Let's have a drink," Ron says, half out of the car already.

"But don't you think we ought to —"

"Now, now. Quit worrying so much. Everything's going to be okay. Come on. We have plenty of time. You're covered on all of this."

In the restaurant's cool interior, I stumble in the darkness, almost falling as I miss a step. We sit at the bar and order drinks. Ron lights a cigarette and silently fingers his glass.

"Is there something we ought to be doing?" I ask.

"I told you not to worry."

"Maybe I ought to call the home office."

"The home office is taken care of," Ron replies, a trace of contempt in his voice.

"What do you mean, taken care of?"

"I mean they have no problem."

"No problem with what, who?"

"No problem with you."

"But they don't even know about me. As far as they're concerned, for the time being I've just vanished. Unless Fred has called already and told them where I am."

"We must assume that has happened."

"What do you mean, we must assume? Why must we assume that?"

"Because that is the most natural course of events. That is what would happen. Such an occurrence would take place quite logically in the typical corporate episode of this sort."

Ron's speech has, inexplicably, taken on a sharply different quality. Perhaps it was the alcohol.

"Episode of this sort? There are no corporate episodes of

this sort. This is, to say the least, a unique and unprecedented happening."

"Whether it is unique and unprecedented is not for us to say. In fact, we don't even have any business speculating about the nature of this incident. Things often happen under the corporate tent, so to speak, that cannot be readily explained but that are proven by subsequent circumstances to be entirely necessary, well planned, and well executed."

We order more drinks. It is clear now that Ron is no ordinary chauffeur, something I suspected when I was sitting beside him in the car.

The drinks arrive. We sit silently for a long time. My vision improves gradually in the dim light, and for the first time I notice Ron's outsized hands — the hands of a wrestler, strong, hard, covered with scars. Yet the skin of his face is smooth, thin, and almost translucent, without whiskers, the skin of a baby. A most unusual chauffeur. A most unusual man.

"Okay, Ron, what's it all about?" I ask, my voice so loud it surprises me.

But Ron's expression gives up nothing. His face is serious, and his eyes are fixed on the bottles behind the bar as if he hasn't heard me. The muscles of his jaws are tight, and he appears to be concentrating on a problem of enormous complexity. He begins speaking in a low voice, halting and almost shy.

"When I first came to the corporation eighteen years ago, I, like yourself, found many things unexplained. I had come from another world — an entirely different world, a world of death and anger — and when I arrived at the corporation, I asked a lot of questions — too many questions, I am sure. I wanted to know why the corporation was organized the way it was, why it had so many rules, and why so many rules seemed to be stupid or useless. I wanted to know why some people were promoted and others were not, why we were not allowed to criticize the way things were done, why certain basic decisions were made about our products, how they were designed, and how they were sold. Oh, I asked a lot of questions and I spent a great amount of time speculating about these things, things I had no right to be concerned about. All of this consumed time that I might better have spent improving my performance.

"This period of endless questioning and endless rumination about the many mysteries that confronted me lasted for several years. Then one day I met a man — an older man who had been with the Company for many years — and my entire life and outlook toward the corporation changed."

Ron drains the last of the martini from his glass and orders another. He does not continue immediately, and I say nothing to interrupt his train of thought. He remains sitting silently, rubbing a finger over the rim of his glass, his mind a thousand miles away.

By the time the next round of drinks arrives, I have almost forgotten about him. I am thinking what I will tell Marlott about this when I get back. The story will be deliciously incredible — kidnaped by the Chairman, abandoned without instructions at the Los Angeles airport, and so forth. My innocence will be hilariously upsetting to him, because the Company is equipped to deal only with guilt. The more I think about my first meeting with Marlott, the funnier it all seems. I begin to laugh, then catch myself. I get up from the barstool, reeling slightly.

"Gotta go to the men's room. Back in a second," I tell Ron. He seems to take no notice, continuing to stroke the rim of his glass and gaze at the bottles ahead of him.

Funny, funny, funny. A disquieting little mystery — the sudden disappearance of a speechwriter in the company of the Chairman. In the Chairman of the Company? No. I stumble against another of the invisible steps. Well, in any event, it will be worth seeing Marlott's face, seeing how he takes it when I tell him this fantastic story.

When I return from the men's room, Ron is gone. I am stunned. Abandoned twice. An abandonment within an abandonment. The man was not who he said he was, anyway. An industrial spy, perhaps? A nonindustrial spy, perhaps? I stand there in a state of drunken confusion. It dawns on me that one or two people are staring at me. They may be confederates of Ron's. On the other hand, they may have nothing to do with any of this. I take my place on the stool in front of me. The bartender appears, smiling pleasantly. I order another drink and continue musing and chuckling to myself about all that has happened. There is no time or sense of place, only the vague consciousness of the smiling bartender, of full glasses being set before me and empty ones returned. A rock group has arrived, and its music can be felt vibrating the glass in my hand. The music gives me a headache, and panic begins to reach out and grip every part of my body. I can't think straight about any of this. The way out of the bar seems as obscure as the way in. Shaking, I get up to leave, flinging all of the money in my wallet onto the bar. Then everything goes blank, and I feel the hard floor rise up to strike me.

4

I AWAKE IN A HOTEL ROOM more opulent than any I have
ever seen before. The bed is twice the normal size and much
too soft for comfort. The walls are covered with pale green
fabric. Badly hung over, I spill out of bed onto the generous
gold carpet, which almost threatens to engulf me. I make my
way to the window, part the drapes, and peer outside. The
room is high up, perhaps thirty stories or so, and I am suddenly dizzy. I reel backward and plunge into a chair. I try
to remember how I got into the room, but I remember nothing except the long flight to Los Angeles and the ride to the
bar.

Did all of this really happen or is it another hallucination?
Where am I? Is this some kind of clever corporate test? If it
is, I have obviously failed. I have failed the test of modera-
tion, one of the principal corporate requirements. I have
failed to resist the temptation of overindulgence, hardly a
major offense in any other scale of values, but not to be tol-

erated in one of the largest corporations in the country. Perhaps my indiscretion has been captured on videotape, to be shown to a select audience of company psychologists and personnel people in the soft, whirring ambience of a private conference room. I can visualize the scene. Absolute silence, and when the lights are turned on, a grave and embarrassed clearing of throats. The first comments would be tentative and tolerant. An understandable aberration that could be blamed on the long, stressful plane ride in the company of the Chairman. It is obvious that the subject displayed a certain failure of self-discipline under circumstances that were unusual and that could hardly have been anticipated. "Well, I couldn't agree more with that analysis," someone would say. "The positive aspect of this incident is that such minor character flaws are, in our experience, usually correctible with a carefully conceived and executed program of rehabilitation therapy. The first step, I suggest" — so the discussion would go — "is to confront the subject employee with his conduct in a way that is not ego destructive, to leave him with the feeling that overall, he is a good and valued employee who has shown one distressful but important failing: the inability to conduct himself with dignity and restraint in all situations, whether or not his identity could be connected with the Company's good name."

The entire discussion, as I imagine it here in the hotel room, is absurd. But then, so is my being here. I am just about to drift back to sleep when the phone rings.

"Sir, your limousine will be in front of the hotel to pick you up for the trip to the airport in half an hour," says a soft, sensual woman's voice.

"Just a minute. Just a minute. Who is this, anyway?" I shout into the receiver. But no one is there.

I dress hurriedly, noticing that my suit, hanging all alone in the spacious closet, is neatly pressed, showing none of the effects of the long plane trip and the hours spent drinking in the bar.

The lobby is nearly deserted. Stiff functionaries stand nearly motionless by the registration desk and the bell captain's station. The place reminds me of an office. It is as if it were an outpost of the corporate headquarters — the same artificial silence, the same tasteless opulence.

The limousine that pulls up outside is one of our own company cars, unmistakable in its outdated extravagance. A huge chunk of metal weighing more than two tons, with windows that are cut at odd angles, mock coach lanterns, various slivers of gleaming chrome fixed to the sides like mother-of-pearl on a cigarette case. The color combination is atrocious — lavender with a tan vinyl top. Altogether, it reminds me of the most elaborate casket offered by an expensive funeral home. At the wheel is a gorgeous blonde who is staring through the layers of glass that separate us with a smile as innocent as a nun's. No mistake about it, this is my chauffeur.

"Hi, my name is Celia Carter," she says when I am beside her in the car. She pounces on the accelerator and we are off on the busy boulevard.

"The first thing we'll do is check back at the office before we take off for the airport," she says. "Is that okay with you?"

"Do I have any choice?"

"Not really, but it does seem like a sensible plan, doesn't it? You never know when there might be an emergency, somebody really important trying to get in touch with us."

"Eminently reasonable," I say, trying to decide if anybody so beautiful can really be a company official. It seems more than likely that she is playing a role, just as Ron played a role in the bar a few hours (or was it a few days?) ago. There is a facade of competence about her, a thin layer of briskness that hints at an explosive sensuality. The two qualities are almost in balance — the Harvard MBA and the natural seductress. They are, I realize, not mutually exclusive, but the combination is uncommon.

It is another cookie-cutter building, a glass and aluminum confection dripping with expensive draperies, carpeting, ashtrays, potted plants, and elevators as fast as they are quiet.

When the door to the elevator opens, we walk down a long corridor to a turn guarded by one of the Company's beefy security men posing as a receptionist.

"Hello, Miss Carter, how are you today?"

"Fine, Roger, just fine."

The door to Celia's office is locked, which seems a bit odd to me. When I follow her inside, she closes and locks it again. Much to my amazement, there is no secretary — just an office that seems to stretch interminably toward a huge expanse of glass that looks out on the smoggy skyline.

It takes us forever to cross the ocean of carpet. Celia motions me to a chair in front of her desk, a desk larger than the Chairman's, which strikes me as a most indiscreet extravagance. She puts her hand under the desktop and the curtains close with a businesslike *whir*. A slightly pink light, soft and almost misty, fills the room from hidden lamps.

"Like a drink?"

"Uh, I don't think so, no, not really."

"Why not? As I said, we've got plenty of time. Three hours before boarding time, in fact. What's the problem? You a real company man?"

"Not really. It's just that I'm not thirsty."

"Not thirsty? That's quite funny, you know. You do have a sense of humor behind that rather serious exterior. Why don't you relax for a few moments? You have been under a lot of strain, you know, and I'm sure the Chairman wouldn't mind if you relaxed for a few minutes before you flew back."

She said Chairman with a capital C. I know that she is dangerous, not to be trusted, possibly even vicious, but there is a certain self-destructive quality in me that tends to overlook such danger signals, especially when I realize I may be in deep trouble anyway.

We drink, amiably and calmly at first, with a tempo that increases as the afternoon wears on. The pink light becomes more diffuse, the room becomes warmer, and the conversation grows more and more personal. I was right about one thing. It was a Harvard MBA, immediately following a bachelor's in economics at Smith. Then a couple of years with a computer software company in Connecticut before the big jump to the top of the Fortune 500.

Everything, she confides in a way that is not the least offensive, is going according to the plan she devised during her sophomore year, a plan she worked out on her own but submitted to her father for his enthusiastic endorsement.

Well, that is all very nice, but what about me? she wants to know. At this, I open up in a way that even I find surprising, gathering speed as the alcohol tightens its grip, talking like a maniac about the Company, what happened before, my years in the navy, college, childhood. I find myself saying things to this perfect stranger that I had never said to anyone before, including myself.

To all of this, Miss Carter is most agreeable and understanding, sympathetic, and supportive in a way that is part maternal, part best friend. How could anyone so beautiful be so smart and sensitive, so wise and experienced, yet so young? It is all a wonderful conclusion to the nightmare trip that is about to end.

"Can't you relax a little?" Celia asks.

"It's hard for me. I have a very tough job."

"Tell me about it."

"What do you want to know?"

"Everything." Celia seems really interested.

"Well, I write speeches for the top executives. Maybe it's a bit misleading to say top, because in theory we could be called upon to write for any one of twenty-three company vice presidents, the President, the vice chairman."

"Even the Chairman?"

"Yes, the Chairman."

"I find that very exciting," Celia says. Can she really mean it? Maybe so. It's a grim thought, but somehow I like it.

"Well, what kind of speeches are they?"

"Junk, useless stuff. Speeches for groups of businessmen attending conventions, or Rotary clubs, or economic clubs of this city or that. The audience is made up of a lot of businessmen. Quite a lot of them give speeches, too, so there is a kind of cross-fertilization, a lot of repetition."

"Yes, but I would imagine some important things are said, too," Celia replies. She has moved over to the couch and pats a cushion next to her, inviting me to move closer. I do.

"Please go on," she says in a soft voice, her face now only a few inches from mine.

"You don't really want to hear this, do you?" I ask, suspecting some kind of trap.

"Of course I do. This is very interesting. You have to admit your job is kind of exotic."

I've had just enough to drink to believe her. So, like a fool, I continue, full of myself and my newfound importance.

"Well, all the speeches are about the same length, twenty to thirty-five minutes. They cover pretty much the same ground, too — economic forecasts, the state of the industry, a description of the Company's activities, and so forth.

"You don't read much about them in the newspapers or hear them on television because — to be quite frank — they rarely say anything worth reporting.

"Oh, once in a while there will be an announcement of a

plant expansion or a new product, and that kind of thing will get into the newspaper.

"But for the most part, these speeches are dead the moment they are given. The fact is, they're dead even before they are given. If you went to hear one of them, you would see some of the audience rush up to the speaker after the speech. They stand there congratulating him on his incisive observations, or original thoughts, or worthwhile suggestions. But we know they do this only for political reasons."

Celia has her arm around me now and I'm finding it hard to concentrate. In fact, I've forgotten what I've told her.

"There sure are a lot of opportunists in business, aren't there?" Celia is saying into my left ear, her voice almost a whisper. Somehow it strikes me as a very important observation, very original.

"Well, anyway," I continue, picking up the train, "sometimes a speech that's considered very superior will be reprinted in an attractive brochure with the Company's logo on it. This can be very expensive, maybe several thousand dollars.

"The reason this happens is that someone upstairs puts out the word that there's a big demand for this speech and that we need to print at least five thousand copies just to fill requests.

"But after they're printed, it develops that we don't get any requests at all. The brochures just sit there in a cardboard box on top of some filing cabinet. Marlott once had five thousand copies of a speech printed. But only two of them were given out — to the President himself. He liked the speech. He gave it."

"What a waste, what an incredible waste!" Celia murmurs. She is now sitting on my lap, both of her arms around my neck, and she is showing more interest in my job than anyone I've ever met.

"But the worst thing is that it's so hard to write speeches

that say anything, because you're not allowed to write anything that might be considered the least bit controversial or provocative.

"Of course you can't write anything remotely political. You can't write anything that might be considered offensive to stockholders or unions, or women or minorities, or other businessmen or farmers or teetotalers, or just about anybody you can name."

I'm vaguely aware at this point that I've had way, way too much to drink and that I've lost control of the situation — if I ever had it. But I feel good. I hardly pause. It's the best chance I've ever had to talk about the horrors of corporate speechwriting.

"I still don't know why it's so bad," Celia purrs into my ear. By this time we are on the floor, and her hands have mounted a serious exploration of my body.

"Well, let me tell you. The problem is that your speech is fair game for anyone. And everyone imagines he — or she — is a writer. Didja get that? He or she. Pretty sensitized, wouldn't you say?"

"Very sensitized." Celia agrees. She continues sensitizing me, using techniques I've never heard of before, let alone encountered.

"Well, the speech goes out for clearance — copies to everyone and his brother — to Marketing, Legal, Finance, Engineering, and so forth. They're all given a chance to comment, correct mistakes, take things out, and add things. The speech is up for grabs.

"Then the clearance copies start coming back with comments — lovely comments like 'Bullshit,' or 'Ridiculous,' or 'Says who?' Sometimes whole paragraphs are deleted, whole pages, in fact.

"This process goes on and on. Sometimes as many as a dozen drafts are written for a single speech. Each of these must be copied and sent to the dozen or so clearance points.

"So, at one time, maybe three or four drafts are out for clearance. This means that just as the Engineering Department finally returns its copy of draft number three with its suggested changes, it receives draft number four."

Celia doesn't seem to be paying as close attention as she had when I first started. She has stripped down to her underwear and is in the process of removing my pants when I think of more to say. I am so eager to get it off my chest that I find myself pushing her hands away, urging her to let me finish.

"It's always a great joke to describe this at cocktail parties," I continue, "because people think it's glamorous, fascinating.

"They seem to believe that we spend hours locked in weighty discussions with the Chairman or President, solving the political problems of the industry, the country, or even the world.

"They seem to think that the man who writes the speeches and the man who gives them have a very close and informal relationship. They have this picture of us pacing back and forth together in deep philosophical discussion, arguing, making jokes, refining points, discussing the meaning of words.

"Well, nothing could be further from the truth. The fact is that we rarely see our so-called clients. We can write the entire speech from the first draft to the last without seeing them at all."

At this point, Celia seems to have lost interest altogether. We are on the floor together, naked, doing close and intimate things to each other, probing, touching, feeling, breathing, tasting. Celia is very excited now, her breath coming in short gasps, and I am finally losing interest in what I was saying.

"Pressure very great. Great tension. Worse than newspaper deadlines. Nobody can imagine."

"I can imagine," Celia whispers. "Can you imagine this?"

Everything comes apart at once. We are lost in each other's body, lost in the soft carpet, struggling and gasping as we roll across the room. Time and space merge in a dream that seems endless. I feel as if I am losing consciousness, caught in some kind of sexual trance.

When I awake, Miss Carter — Celia, as I had called her only moments before — is sitting behind her desk busily writing on a yellow memo pad. Two other women are in different stages of undress. All seem oblivious to the fact that I am lying on the floor naked. The other women are calmly putting on their clothes, and Miss Carter says, without looking up from her memo pad, "Why don't you get dressed now, please. It's almost time for us to leave. If you don't hurry, you won't make the plane."

On the ride to the airport, the last vestige of Celia Carter, seductress, has vanished. The Harvard Business School is in command now. She advises me to be sure to file an expense account as soon as I get back to the home office, since she will be asked to review it and she likes to keep current on such things.

Current, indeed. Is this the woman I was lying naked with only a few minutes ago? Corporations have a remarkable capacity for creating the perfectly schizoid employee, one who can adopt any one of several personalities to fit the occasion without a moment's notice. A perfectly trained schizoid, Celia, and I am totally under her control. How can anyone abandon such intimacy so quickly and completely? I know that there is no use at all in trying to remind her that less than an hour ago, we were the closest of friends.

The plane is an air-conditioned womb, soft and safe, tight and comforting. I drink heavily on the flight back, so much that the stewardess finally refuses to serve me any more, making some charming remark about looking after my health. I am exhausted, drunk, and in a state of total confusion when I board the taxi for the ride home. I will try to sober up, try to unravel the mystery that has just been played out. I know that I have had too much to drink. I know that I am confused and angry. But I know, too, that I won't sleep until some questions are answered.

5

At our first meeting since my return, Marlott is more enigmatic than ever. I imagine I look as if I have just come off a three-day drunk, but nothing is said about my appearance.

"Have a nice trip?" he asks, not looking up from the pad he is scribbling on. Why is it that in a corporation, no superior will look at you when he speaks? He is always writing things on yellow legal pads, notes and observations and orders of monumental and immediate importance, always looking too busy to be distracted by the presence of underlings. It is, of course, a pose designed to humiliate. But then there is always the possibility, remote but real enough to be disturbing, that he is truly occupied with matters so important that they can't be ignored for a second.

Marlott seems unperturbed. But I know that his equanimity can be a dangerous guise. The calmer and less distracted he may seem, the more malicious he may suddenly become.

"Everything all right here?" I ask.

"Of course, of course. Everything is first rate. So tell me, how did you enjoy your little trip with the Chairman?"

At that point, Marlott drops his pressing business. His face is expressionless, his voice empty. This is the most dangerous game in the corporation, making one's way through water that is so smooth, so devoid of temperature and feeling, current and obstruction, that you can't even be sure it is there.

"Well, yes. It was all right, I guess. No, it was fine. It was really good."

"Really good."

"Well, it was fine. There wasn't anything extraordinary about it, really. Nothing very exciting happened."

"Nothing very exciting."

"No. Nothing very exciting. I mean, it was an ordinary trip to California with the Chairman. Nothing out of the ordinary happened."

"But you've never taken a trip to California with the Chairman before."

"That's certainly true, Mike. But what I mean is that it's the kind of experience most people would have on a trip to California with the Chairman."

"Well, I'm glad you think so. Sometimes these things appear to be well within the parameters of normality when in fact they are not. There is really no way of knowing at the time. Sometimes trips of this sort can have surprising consequences, and other times they don't seem to mean much of anything."

"I'm not sure I know what you mean by that, Mike."

"Oh, don't worry about it. Can you give me a new draft of the Chairman's speech by Wednesday?"

"Sure, Mike. I'll even beat that deadline if I can."

"Good. See you later." Mike turns back to his scribbling. I ease my way out of his office, backing up like some Oriental slave. Here again I see the danger of the entire game. Not to appear too subservient, because such a pose will be seen as false. But not lacking in respect, either. The problem is, one supervisor's standard of respect is different from another's. Conrad and I talk about this endlessly, agreeing that it is probably difficult to err on the side of excess. We joke about practicing and perfecting the ideal executive shuffle, a mixture of camaraderie and deference that would be ingenious in its perfect balance.

Dr. Mirsch eats chocolate chip cookies while I describe the trip to Los Angeles. It's not necessary to embroider the story; it stands on its own. Gathering speed as the mystery of these events deepens, my account takes on the breathless style of a small boy telling his mother about some neighborhood fracas he has just survived. "And then . . . and then . . . and then."

But Dr. Mirsch is not to be moved.

"What do you think of all this?" he asks.

"What do you mean, what do I think of this?"

"Why do you ask me that question? You know what I mean when I ask, 'What do you think of this?' "

"I know what you mean, but I think it's a stupid question. What am I supposed to think of all this? It's like asking, 'What do you think about life?' The point is, it happened. The whole question is why? What I 'think' of it is not important. The real question is, why did all this happen?"

"Then you are sure that it all happened?"

I turn around to stare in disbelief. His mouth is full of cookies. Someone, some insurance company, is paying him seventy dollars an hour for eating chocolate chip cookies and asking, "What do you think of this?"

Silence takes over. Hostility and hatred fill the room, but I know the hostility and hatred are all mine. My interrogator is without feeling, a fat robot stuffed with cookies and Freud. Trained to the nth degree through long years of apprenticeship to dispense exquisitely timed silences and infinitely subtle questions, part of an arcane "science" understood and practiced by only a few thousand cognoscenti who meet every few months in expensive spas or on luxury cruise ships to exchange the latest gossip about the mystery of the human mind.

The silence lingers. This time I am not going to capitulate. Nor will I respond to his inane question challenging my perception of what happened.

"After all, you might have had too much to drink." Of course, he would never say I was drunk. He was trained not to say anything so straightforward. Perhaps all of this was in a glossary of acceptable comments. Maybe there are only twelve authorized comments in the manual of the American Psychoanalytic Association.

"Of course I had too much to drink, for Christ's sake," I shout. I catch myself trembling and lower my voice. "But the events as I described them happened. Naturally, you see things through a glass darkly when you've been drinking, but that doesn't mean that everything you remember is a hallucination, does it?"

"Well, what do you think about that?"

Silence, again. I look at my watch. I am grateful to the inventor of the fifty-minute hour, the man or woman who decided that human beings could stand no more than fifty minutes of this kind of torture.

"Well, the time is up," says Dr. Mirsch. "We'll continue this at our next session. Friday?"

"Friday."

In the corridor on the way to my office, I bump into Barbara Burdoch, looking more Harvard Business Schoolish than ever, not unlike the woman in Los Angeles. Her face has taken on the semismile of semicondescension, not obvious enough to be offensive, but meant to signal total self-confidence in one's ability, the total confidence one enjoys from one's superiors. Skillfully applied, the semismile can shake the equilibrium of one's competitors, because the smile says either "I know something about my place in the organization that you don't know" or, more disturbing, "I know something about *your* place in the organization that you don't know." Whatever its purpose, Barbara has now mastered this much-envied smile. With the smile, the purposeful stride, the deepened voice, the look of an animal preparing to attack that seems to be her natural expression, Barbara strikes me now not as a smart young woman with ambition, but as a dangerous adversary who possesses the will and the means to destroy me.

"How was your trip to Los Angeles? How did you get along with our beloved Chairman?"

"The Chairman and I got along fine. As for the trip, it was just normal. Nothing unusual. Altogether pleasant, as a matter of fact."

I have to be positive, but not too positive. I have to be casual, but not too casual. All meaning, I know, resides not so much in what is said — because little of meaning is ever said — but in demeanor, inflection, attitude. These people have been trained to detect every shading of attitude, and a positive attitude toward the Company and toward one's superiors is the surest proof of loyalty, the employee's first and most important armor.

"Yes, it was really quite a good trip. It was a good opportunity to meet with the Chairman and have a good talk. It was good to get out of the office for a short time and be exposed to another environment. And, of course, it's also good to be back."

She says nothing. We walk a little farther, then she turns to go into her office.

"Well, I'm glad you had such a good trip. I hope you'll tell me more about it when you have time."

Do people really talk that way here in the corporation? Of course they do. It is, it seems to me, an extension of the language used by Dr. Mirsch and his colleagues. A sanitized kind of language in which all emotion, all opinion, all the feel, taste, and smell of human experience have been removed. This corporate language has all the sterility of a computer language. It is corporate BASIC, a language that can be learned just as one can learn to talk to a computer. Using it, one finds that it is precise and unforgiving. Whenever one departs from the system's glossary, there is no response. This language is special and narrow; it works superbly when it is put to the purpose for which it was designed. But that purpose is technical and restricted, the purpose of communicating business. Beyond that, one has to fall back upon human language, the really important nonverbal language of the face and the body, the instantaneous narrowing of the eyes or the widening of the semismile by a few millimeters. This is the language that contains the secrets of one's corporate place and of one's corporate fate.

Lunch with Conrad is enlivened by my excited account of the trip to Los Angeles. It is a story that needs no exaggeration, and Conrad is appropriately impressed.

"God," he keeps saying. "Jesus. I can't believe it." This is one of his many charms — to fall in fully with your panic and to accept completely your predictions of imminent disaster.

When I finish, he stirs his coffee quietly and shakes his head.

"Just remember what I've said before, old boy. A very wise man told me once, 'Ninety-nine percent of paranoia is justified.' "

"You mean you accept it? You think it all happened, just that way?"

He looks indignant.

"Of course I accept it. Why shouldn't I? Stranger things have happened, I suppose, but this is strange enough. Sure I accept it. But I have no idea why it happened or what it means."

6

If blanders and stein really exist, what happened to their names beneath the buttons on my intercom? Those two little slips of paper were the only solid evidence I had that they existed at all. They may have been pointed out to me one day in the corridor, shadowy figures on their way to the cafeteria, but I'm not sure. I think of them, if I think of them at all, as blips on a radar screen, their existence suspected but unproven. They are certainly corporate, but important questions remain. Function? Status? Reporting to? Now they had disappeared altogether from the screen. Sunk? Changed course? False images?

I smoke and pace, trying to solve the mystery. Gloria can't see me so long as I stick to the path I am on. No one can see me through the open door. But then, no one ever looks inside. My office is hundreds of miles from the nearest regular trade route. It could be years before I am discovered. In the meantime, I must sustain myself on the tropical fruits and small shellfish of bureaucracy. Every morning, the incoming tide of office mail brings an assortment of company communications — reports, memoranda, changes in orders, and new regulations. Tasteless stuff, although it occasionally contains some nourishment. I ingest it slowly, hoping for something new and different. Once or twice a week I receive a telephone call. But these calls are almost always for a man with a similar name in another department.

It's sad that the Company took away our given names and replaced them with initials. Stein and Blanders, for instance, are E. G. Stein and A. K. Blanders. At least that is how their names appeared under my intercom buttons. Perhaps when they were schoolchildren, the records carried them as Edward George Stein and Arthur Kenneth Blanders. But I will never know for sure, because I never saw or heard their given names. Perhaps the Company thought that given names would create problems of association. They can remind people of other Edwards and other Arthurs they have known. The point is that names in themselves might affect business-like relationships between employees.

Of course, following this logic, last names ought to be done away with as well and replaced by a system of numbers. But the Company probably concluded that this would be too cold and impersonal and might cause discontent among the employees. And so, alongside all the doors through the corridors, you will see hundreds of small metal plates with last names preceded by initials. The possible combinations are seemingly endless, and you can amuse yourself by looking for strange and unusual couplings. Apparently the Company frowns upon combinations that are easily identified with given names, because you never see them. An example would be the familiar F. X., for Francis Xavier, so popular with Catholics. That combination would tend to identify its owner's religious preference, something that would certainly be against company policy. Some combinations are harmless but amusing, such as O. K. Progress, which Conrad and I first mistook for a department or an office. Other combinations are possibly scatological, such as B. S. Turner or M. F. Nelson. The parents of these unfortunate functionaries had no way of knowing that changing times would give their children's initials impolite meanings or that these initials themselves would become their children's official corporate names.

Conrad breezes into my office, a gentle giant, soft-spoken, bursting with wit, moving with a doorman's dignity. Overweight, with owlish eyes that peer through thick glasses, he might be an aging sergeant-major in the British army. In his usual way, he smiles while gazing beyond me through the window, studying the gently drifting clouds along the horizon.

"Blanders and Stein are missing," I say.

"Meaning what?"

"Meaning that their names have been removed from my intercom."

Conrad continues gazing at the sky. "You read some great significance into that? It is, perhaps, an omen — two geese silhouetted against the setting sun, perhaps, or the carcass of a chicken found lying next to a pumpkin?"

He can be cruel. Why does he make fun of me now when it is he who has told me, his face full of conviction, that ninety-nine percent of paranoia is justified? My own guess is that the figure should have been more like sixty percent. But then, I have not lived Conrad's fifty years, not quite, nor have I shared his special suffering.

We arrived here only two months apart, and because I had been the first, I adopted a protective attitude toward him. I know this attitude is presumptuous, and I suspect that he resents it. And yet I persist in it. In the first place, it makes me feel important. And second, he seems to welcome it. Surely we need support. Corporations are lonely places; a friend can spell the difference between life and death. But a corporate friend is extremely rare.

The intercom buzzes. It is Marlott. I tense, because I know that this little electric pulse means trouble, possibly big trouble.

"Yes, sir," I say, my voice an embarrassment of sycophancy.

"Can you come see me for a minute? And is Conrad there?"

"Yes."

"Well, bring him along, too. The more, the merrier."

"Be right there, sir."

I look at Conrad. The sad, resigned smile. The slow, gentle sigh of the lost corporate soul. I rise slowly.

"We who are about to die curse you," I say.

We make our way to Marlott's office. Is there any reason why grown people have to report to the principal's office and expose themselves to certain humiliation? No. But that is what we do. We do it because we have to. Because of mortgages. Because of spouses, children, car payments. We pass a mirror, thoughtfully placed in the corridor to let the alert careerist adjust his appearance before reporting to a superior. I look at myself and see the beaten, slumped reflection of corporate man, the worried face, the sagging shoulders, the look of passive despair. Is this, I ask myself, the thing the Lord God made to have dominion over land and sea? Only two hundred years before this, Indians stalked game on the very spot where this building stands, or silently pursued their enemies through forest paths as dark as night. We have come a long way since then, I think. Now we worry about the crease of our trousers, the tenor of our voices. The love song of corporate man is not "Do I dare to eat a peach?" as T. S. Eliot put it, but "Do I dare even to think of eating a peach?" Because they know what you are thinking, and thoughts can be used against you.

Marlott sits in towering superiority behind a giant walnut desk. The desk cost five thousand dollars, which is more than his father made a year for laying sidewalks in Trenton, New Jersey, when Marlott was born there in 1918.

Marlott does not look up when we enter. Conrad and I know that obeisance is expected, but we have never quite understood what form it should take. Should we perhaps say "Good afternoon, sir. How may we serve you?" Obviously not; we realize that sounds false and strained. And yet that is what is expected of us, so why not say it? Or should we choose false familiarity, hoping to conceal the chasm between us. "Hi, Mike. How's it going?" No. That would never do, either.

We are relieved; Marlott only wants us to schedule our vacations. On the way back to our offices, Conrad and I talk about our hatred of him, our favorite subject. Marlott makes us very nervous. But we agree that we would be very nervous even if Marlott weren't in the picture.

Back in my office, I pace and smoke. Giving up on the speech I'm writing, I decide to consult the house oracle. I will talk to the strange but fantastically wise seer of speechwriters, Schwartz. Schwartz is the dean of the Company's speechwriters, a man who wrote successfully for the Founder. His five greatest speeches have been published between covers of dark blue cloth embossed with gold. A gnomelike man, completely bald with pale blue eyes, Schwartz now occupies one of the best offices on the floor, shows up for work only two or three hours a day, and is known to have written only one speech this year. The Chairman himself is so in awe of him that he never changes a word of his speeches. And once, while giving a lecture to business students at Yale, the Chairman shyly pointed out Schwartz, slumped in embarrassment in the third row, as the real author of his remarks.

I rush down the corridor to Schwartz's office, and I am delighted to find him at his desk, his back to the door, gazing out the window. There is nothing on his desk, not a paper or a book. On the credenza is a water carafe and a picture of his daughter, who has been studying snakes in New Guinea for ten or twelve years.

Hearing me enter, Schwartz turns and smiles his sad smile. I explain my problem, hoping that he doesn't detect the panic behind my calm manner.

A little help, that's all. Take a look at the outline. Maybe a suggestion. Some ideas. Schwartz motions me to a seat. I slump deeply into his dark brown leather couch, from which I can see the stern likeness of the Founder encased in a dark oak frame above the desk.

Schwartz studies the outline interminably. The corporate hum clicks off unaccountably, then just as mysteriously resumes at a slightly higher pitch. The deep, sincere voices of executives are heard in the hallway. A door closes nearby. Schwartz, meanwhile, finishes the outline, lays it on the desk thoughtfully, and stares vacantly outside. I know that he is brilliant, or so it is said. Surely, anyone who can write for the Chairman so successfully, who wrote successfully for the Founder and all those who followed him, who can do this without notes or books or research material — simply by staring out the window — such a man must be brilliant.

I wait. Finally, after what seems to be an interminable length of time, Schwartz turns to me, slowly lifts his hands in a gesture of despair, and shrugs.

"What?" I ask anxiously.

"Nothing."

"What do you mean, nothing?"

"There is nothing you can do."

"Meaning what?" I ask, the panic growing.

"It's all been said," Schwartz declares. He gets up from his desk, opens a closet door, puts on his frayed, checked hat, and eases into his dark blue raincoat that badly needs cleaning.

"I'm going now," he says. "You've got a problem. The fact of the matter is, it's all been said. Everything."

Schwartz is right. It has all been said. And very little of it was worth saying in the first place. I go back to the office. The first thing I do is look at the intercom. Thank God! Blanders and Stein are back in their proper places. And why shouldn't they be? The names were never missing in the first place. I had imagined it all. It was one of those little tricks the mind plays on you. And that coat I knew I had taken to the cleaner's. I could remember the look of the clerk who took it. And yet there it is, hanging in my closet. Mirrors. Flashing lights. A figment, a mirage. The failure of a synapse.

Conrad walks through the door, passing by me without looking, and stands against the air-conditioning vent, leaning over to stare at the parking lot ten stories below.

"Nice parking lot," he grumbles. "Lots of style. A fascinating view of the stark industrial landscape, this. Acres of glistening cars, and just over there on the horizon the belching smokestacks of the factory that makes them. This is your life, pal. This is my life. This is everybody's life. Come on. It's time to go to lunch."

We stop at the men's room. Conrad waits outside. The only other person in the men's room is Jim Stuart, who has been with the Company for twenty-eight years. Stuart has gray hair, is overweight, and wears thick, rimless glasses that seem to magnify his eyes, giving him a terrified look. He almost never smiles, but he manages to convey a feeling of friendliness and good will. It is said that he has nine children, three of whom must still be put through college. Perhaps this accounts for his weariness. Yet he is scrupulously polite, with a manner that resembles a department store floorwalker.

"Little cooler out there today," I say. There is little else one can think of saying to Stuart.

Stuart gives me his confidential look, tosses the paper towel into the wastebasket, and bends over. He sweeps his gaze along the floor under the stalls, searching for feet. Satisfied that we are alone, he turns and gives me his most courteous look.

"Certainly is, but it's supposed to warm up for the weekend."

"Fine. Fine. Listen, Jim," I say, "what do you know about Blanders and Stein?"

"What do you mean, what do I know? Am I supposed to know anything?"

"Not really. But what I mean is, are they still on this floor? Has there been a change in their status or something?"

"Not that I know of. But then, I'm not in a position to know. Everything is just fine with them, as far as I know. But you really ought to talk to someone else if you're interested. Well, listen, take care. It's good to see you. I don't see much of you these days. Have you been out sick?"

"No, Jim. I haven't been out sick. I've been here every day."

"Well, anyway, have a happy day." Stuart's face looks like one of the smiling faces that teachers draw on a pupil's best work.

Conrad and I take our usual circuitous route to the cafeteria where we eat. This is not the cafeteria that others in our department use. It is one we chose to avoid them. It has taken us a long time to hit upon a route that offers the least possible risk of our encountering anyone. We follow a long corridor almost to its end, descend a flight of stairs to the next floor, and get on a small freight elevator seldom used by anyone in our department. When we reach the basement, we start walking along a long corridor with cream-colored walls and a gray tile floor. The corridor makes three sharp turns before we reach our destination, and at each of these turns, large mirrors have been placed to allow pedestrians to see approaching electrified carts that speed through the basement. The route is little traveled. It is also long; it takes us ten minutes to get from our floor to the cafeteria. The basement corridor is a tunnel connecting the headquarters of the Company with a smaller building housing a subsidiary operation. The tunnel is a couple of blocks long. Occasionally, we pass doors with signs that describe the offices inside, obscure departments and sections such as Planning and Interdepartmental Communications or Personnel Reconciliation and Deployment. Once Conrad, who is bolder than I am about such things, tried to open some of these doors, but they were all locked.

"Dummy departments." Conrad snorted. "Probably all CIA."

$$7$$

"How long have you been feeling this fear?"

Dr. Mirsch has settled into his usual place, an easy chair a couple of feet from my right shoulder as I lie on the couch.

"Oh, it's hard to say exactly. Maybe six months. But it's been growing, this fear."

This is our third session. It's too early to tell what I think of this psychiatrist, but he is forbidding. He seems fiftyish, with thinning blond hair, a growing paunch, and teeth that are too perfect to be real. He comes highly recommended, a teacher of analytic acolytes, the author of several books and a hundred learned articles. Two diplomas hang on the wall, both from the University of Vienna. My first impressions are that he has the brain of a Metternich and the manners of a truck driver. For instance, my appointment is just after his dinner hour. This means that invariably he enters the room with a coffee cup and some kind of dessert in his hands. He chews and swallows loudly while I strain to remember when my brother broke his arm thirty years ago. It has occurred to me that this aggressively displayed appetite may be some new therapeutic device, meant to send juice flowing through my synapses or some such thing. Once, leaning over, he spilled coffee on my shoulder. He said nothing in apology and I said nothing, either. Finally, he broke the silence.

"What do you think of that?"

"What?"

"The little accident."

"What little accident?"

"The coffee spill."

"Oh, that. Well, frankly, nothing."

"Nothing?"

"Nothing."

"An accident, yes?"

"Yes, an accident." There was a long pause.

"Go on, please."

Today Dr. Mirsch is not eating. Perhaps he has decided to zero in on the fear thing, hoping finally to pin it to the cork wall above the couch and mount it like a trophy. For this, he cannot allow himself to be distracted by food or drink.

"Fear. What is this nameless fear?"

"I don't know. You name it."

"That is not my responsibility. It is your responsibility. Everyone is responsible for his own fear. What are you afraid of, or who?"

We have talked about this before, and I have told him who I am afraid of. He cannot have forgotten, because he has such a phenomenal memory.

"You know perfectly well."

"I know what you've told me, but I want to hear you say it again."

"Marlott."

"And why are you afraid of Marlott? Do you think he's going to fire you or demote you?"

I have to be careful with this. It is a reasonable question, and I have to answer as honestly as I can.

"Not really, but he can make things very tough for me."

"How can he do that?"

To my own surprise, I find myself unable to answer. It is something hidden, some imagined quality in Marlott's eyes and hands. I know that Marlott is a killer, but I can't explain how I know this. Certainly I can't provide the scientific evidence that Dr. Mirsch seems to demand.

Silence. An interminable silence. Some purists would allow the entire fifty minutes to pass in silence rather than rend the invisible curtain. At seventy dollars an hour, such silence is expensive.

"May I suggest you are afraid you will be humiliated?"

"Yes, of course. But how? There are probably a hundred different ways, but I have no clear idea which way he might choose."

"Well, let me tell you. When you walk into his office, this person of authority is sitting there in a way that may remind you of fears you had a long time ago. You are, perhaps, afraid of wetting your pants."

This is outrageous. I almost burst into laughter. Can this whole elaborate corporate system be reduced to one simple fear — the fear of wetting one's pants?

"No, I don't think that's it."

"Well, let's leave this question open and continue at our next session," Dr. Mirsch says, reaching for a box of cookies on a table near his chair.

8

A MEETING OF THE speech committee is held every Tuesday. This committee was established to discuss upcoming speeches and make assignments, consider speech themes, and give Marlott a chance to preside over additional meetings — one of his favorite pastimes. Five people are present: Marlott, three speechwriters, and Marlott's secretary, Marian.

"Okay, gentlemen," Marlott says, "and ladies. We are going to talk about one thing and one thing alone — how to make this year's suppliers speech the best ever. Any ideas about a theme?"

The search for new themes goes on continually, but the search never seems to produce results. Most suggestions are rejected out of hand. They have not been tried before, they are too controversial, not "appropriate," to use one of Marlott's favorite words, and so forth. Sometimes a new theme is tried, but almost always it is rejected by our superiors or so festooned with their own thoughts that whatever theme existed in the first place is destroyed. In their final form, none of these speeches ever has a theme.

"How about corporate responsibility?" suggests Honigman, the most junior speechwriter and the one who is always the first to volunteer. "We could take Schwartz's famous speech on corporate responsibility at Yale. That's one of the five great speeches in this Company's history, you know. We could update it with some of the current social data and provide some really valuable new insights that can get us a good deal of favorable attention. We can get input from Schwartz himself, and there is some good stuff on this in the *Harvard Business Review*'s October issue, to mention only one of the things I've read on it recently."

"What do you think of that?" Marlott asks, turning to me.

"It's interesting," I say, wincing at my weak response. "We certainly should give it a close look. Depending on how it's handled, it could be a great success. But it's a tricky subject, and it could give us some real problems in the end."

I have learned exactly how to handle questions like this. When I first began at the Company seven years ago, I made the mistake of meeting such questions directly, with clear, unambiguous answers. But within a short time, paying close attention to my colleagues' style, I learned that direct answers were considered gauche and even disruptive. Firm opinions, clearly expressed, can cause endless trouble. For one thing, they give opponents something solid to chew on, a target for disagreement or ridicule. But the greatest danger of clarity is that it is recoverable. It can be recalled to be used against the speaker. Clear expression can become a powerful weapon in the hands of one's enemies.

"Well," Marlott asks, his face showing a sudden hint of darkness, "what do you think ought to be our theme for this speech?" I know I have gone too far in responding to Honigman's suggestion.

"Oh, it isn't that I dislike Jack's idea," I reply. "In fact, it's got a lot of merit. Maybe as a modus operandi, we ought to use it as a working theme and see where we end up."

I have recovered some ground. And I know I have successfully avoided endorsing Honigman's idea. Of course, the speech would probably end up as a disaster, and Honigman would be all too clearly identified with it in the unlikely event that his theme wins approval all the way up the line.

Marlott lights his pipe, knocking some tobacco on his suit. Has he taken too many Darvons, perhaps, or is it just that he is getting old, a little fuzzy around the edges? The friendly fisherman act is to corporate life today what vaudeville was to Edward Albee. It would be easy to feel sorry for Marlott, except that he is powerful, selfish, and cruel.

The discussion drones on. I am watching Barbara Burdoch, our newest writer and the only woman among us. She is thirtyish, with a nose that is too pointed and the high cheekbones of the classic Viennese beauty. The imperfections of her face give it its rare charm. She is tall and big-boned, with a bottom only slightly too large for her build. She wears only corporate clothes — dark tailored suits, dark pumps with closed toes, blouses with high necks, and no jewelry. Her clothes are expensive and tasteful, but she has gone too far on the conservative side, and from a distance she looks more like a librarian than a public relations woman. Her voice is low, almost mannish, her manner friendly but reserved. The initial impression she gives is one of chasteness, but one begins to suspect that this is a masquerade, a pentimento under which lie dazzling layers of sexuality. Sex, more powerful than flannel, asserts itself through the disguise, softly but clearly, like sounds of Mozart from a music box. Again, she reminds me of the woman in Los Angeles.

Who is Barbara Burdoch, and where did she come from? There is the paragraph of biography in the announcement of her appointment: Vassar, a year as a researcher for *Time*, four years as "manager of research and editorial services" for a small company in Maryland, and, finally, public affairs officer for a now-forgotten cabinet officer. It was during that period, or so we have heard, that she was on loan to the White House speechwriting staff for a year or so. Someone called these facts "drop-dead credentials," but Conrad and I have learned to be skeptical. Conrad, in fact, has tried to verify the White House connection, but the people who would know have long since gone off to other jobs and do not return his calls.

Whatever the truth of her background, Barbara Burdoch quickly established herself as a favorite of Marlott and Stover. Marlott smiles a kind of knowing smile and mutters "brilliant" or "outstanding" when her name is mentioned. This, despite the fact that the only speech she is known to have written since she arrived is a ten-minute tribute to a retiring vice president, entirely conventional in its content and style. One important clue to her swift and wholehearted acceptance is her rumored sponsorship by a certain executive vice president, a man more than old enough to be her father. In this, there is no hint at all of a sexual relationship. There is a widespread belief that the vice president is perhaps a distant relative or at least an old friend of her family.

In any event, Barbara Burdoch goes about with an expression that seems to say "I know something you don't know," a pleasant enough expression, if somewhat disturbing.

Now she stirs herself, turns to Marlott, and with her shy smile reveals her idea for the speech theme.

"I think he could really do an impressive job with a speech built on the 'formula for the future' slogan," she says. "We can describe the various elements that make up the Company, offer 'leadership' as the catalyst of our formula, and describe how they all work together to make profits for suppliers and stockholders alike."

"Super!" Marlott fairly shouts. "By George, I think she's

got it!" He turns to us with a triumphant grin and raised eyebrows. "Where have you guys been? This is a mere slip of a girl, and she comes up with just the right theme — just like that!"

We all laugh too loudly. Conrad throws me a furtive look of despair.

"Well, that's it," Marlott declares, turning his triumphant look on me. "What are you working on?"

"The October twenty-third speech for the President."

"Okay. Soon as you get that out of the way, I want to see a draft based on Barbara's idea. Okay?"

"Sure, Mike. I think it's a great idea, incidentally." I avoid meeting Conrad's eyes.

The meeting breaks up. I try to make it back to the office before Conrad can intercept me, but he catches up and pokes me sharply in the neighborhood of my kidneys.

"Great idea, my ass," he says. "What's the matter with you, anyway? You know perfectly well that it's a shitty idea."

I am annoyed. "Look," I say. "You play your game and I'll play mine, and I'll get to Scotland afore ye."

Conrad walks quickly away, not deigning to look back.

9

BARBARA BURDOCH has apparently been appointed the overseer of the suppliers speech. Like so many things that happen in the Company, the event is not announced. We are supposed to assume that the mere display of authority by one of our colleagues proves its legitimacy. There is an exquisite subtlety to this, an important message written in a code everyone is expected to understand. Actually, there are two messages. The first is that the Company is so splendidly disciplined that no one would assume authority arbitrarily. The second is that people must be submissive enough never to question whether authority is legitimate.

This system is efficient. Since authority is constantly shifting from one person to another, the policy of unannounced power saves an enormous number of memos and meetings. Then, too, if putting a person in charge of a certain task proves to be a mistake, the responsibility can be quietly shifted to another person without the embarrassment of a written announcement. Because we are used to these machinations, it is no surprise at all when Barbara walks into my office one day with a number of "suggestions" for the first draft of the suppliers speech. She handles this encounter with finesse, confirming my first impression that she has a sure instinct for moving through the corporate jungles.

"On that suppliers speech," she says, smiling sweetly, "I think it might be a good idea if we stressed the certainty that the Company will return to profitability in the near future. I've been thinking about it, and my own view is that the entire speech should be very upbeat and positive. Wouldn't you agree with that?"

I agree cheerfully and even thank her for the suggestion. I know she must have expected me to. It isn't up to me to question why she is giving me "suggestions" about the speech any more than it is her duty to explain. Her instructions obviously came from Marlott, who knows that under the system's unspoken rules, it would not be proper to tell me about Barbara's new role.

I look at Barbara and wonder how she would be in bed. Without her library clothes, her full hips beneath me, would she continue to assert her authority in a hundred subtle ways? Some of these new corporate women seemed to want dominion over men. As reparations go, it is not an excessive demand, considering how long men held dominion over them. But how far would this dominion extend — to the bedroom as well as the boardroom? Why not? Well, let them have dominion if they want it. Let them learn all about it: from the winning of it to the losing.

Of course, it's entirely possible that once they gain significant power in the corporate world, women will use it differently than men, and more effectively. I think of Gail McKay, the new marketing vice president. During the past few months, I've attended several meetings where she's been in charge. Her performance is impressive — skill, competence, informality, and tact combined in a distinctive style. Her power works in such a way that we hardly know it's there. If we had enough Gail McKays in positions of real authority, it might make a big difference in the corporate atmosphere. It might be closer to cooperation than coercion. It's an encouraging thought; we'll just have to wait and see.

After Barbara leaves with my assurance of full cooperation, I speculate about what's happening to me here. My role is diminishing, but the change is so gradual that it is almost imperceptible. Is all of this a figment? Do I only imagine that Marlott is displeased with me about something? I review the evidence — meetings that I am not invited to. But be fair — were they meetings I needed to attend? What a stupid question! In the Company, one needs to attend as many meetings as possible. One must know all of what is happening, for the worst sin is to reveal ignorance about events, to have to ask questions.

"You didn't know about the issues subcommittee? Oh, well, I thought everybody knew. But I'll be happy to fill you in. Stop in sometime."

No, the signs are unmistakable. Someone up there doesn't like me.

Marlott calls me in for a quick "chat." A "chat," in Marlott's view, is a monologue in which he gives me his "thoughts" about things I ought to be doing, people I should talk to about speeches, various opinions on economic developments and company affairs. When the "chat" is over, Marlott lights his pipe as a signal of dismissal. On this occasion, our "chat" centers on Marlott's ideas for the suppliers speech, which is assuming heroic importance. Marlott talks for about ten minutes, then pulls his tobacco pouch from his top drawer. It is time for me to go.

"Oh, by the way," he says, fumbling in his briefcase, "Stover and I talked about this speech, and I taped the conversation. Here, you should listen to it. He's got some very good ideas."

In Marlott's view, all of our vice president's ideas are good. He is much given to taping conversations with his superiors, probably as a protective device to prevent misunderstandings but also because it flatters them.

Back in the office, I play the tape. Stover is in his usual form, rambling on about sales and products, market shares, and the likelihood of an economic upturn. Marlott is most amiable, laughing uproariously at the slightest attempt at humor, agreeing enthusiastically, volunteering snippets of gossip that he thinks Stover will find titillating.

Suddenly I hear something that makes my hands turn cold. I rewind the tape and play it back.

"So — your friend will have a draft for us in a week?"

"My friend?" Stover asks. "Ha-ha. That's good, Mike. My friend. My friend and your friend. Speaking of our 'friend,' how is the project coming?"

"Right on schedule, sir."

"Good! Keep me informed."

I can't believe what I hear. Why are they referring to me like this? "Friend?" The word, as they say it, is heavy with sarcasm. And what is the project they referred to?

Heart beating fast, I call Conrad on the intercom.

"Come over here right away!" I command.

"What's wrong? Another dog? Borzoi? Poodle? Saint Bernard?"

"Cut the bullshit. This is serious. Get over here right now."

"Okay, I'll be right there."

As soon as he arrives, I play the tape.

Conrad doesn't react immediately. He gets up slowly, walks to the window, and gazes out at the parking lot.

"Play it again, Sam," he says after what seems like a long time.

We play the tape over half a dozen times. At the most critical phrases, we back up and replay it. We turn the volume up as loud as we can, thinking that we might not be hearing the words correctly. We listen with an earplug, but we hear the same words we hear over the speaker.

"What do you make of that?" I ask.

"I don't know," Conrad replies, frowning. "Craziest thing I ever heard. The most astounding thing is the bit about the project. Are you working on some secret project?"

"No. I'm not working on any secret project. And I don't know if anybody is. The point is, it's a project aimed at me."

"But look, if it's aimed at you, why would Marlott give you the tape?"

"Beats me. Maybe he wants to warn me."

"Seems like an indirect way. Why doesn't he just call you in and tell you?"

"I don't know. You never know about him. Maybe it's too many pills. Maybe it's one of his convoluted little strategies. You should remember that he's a stratagem wrapped in a subterfuge inside a caper. His whole life is intrigue and plotting and deceit. My God, how I hate the bastard!"

"Why don't you just go and ask him what it all means?"

"Are you kidding? You can't do that. He would just say, 'Well, of course you're our friend! Is there some reason why you shouldn't be?' And so on and so forth. And as for the project, he would just say, 'Why, the suppliers speech, of course.' "

"Well," Conrad says, turning to go, "it's one of the little mysteries that make this such a fascinating place in which to grow old gracefully. If I get any bright ideas, I'll let you know. But frankly, I'm stumped."

It's a pity this new puzzle has been added to my current stock. I've already been brooding too much on various cor-

porate mysteries, wasting too much time trying to explain incidents like the missing Blanders and Stein name tags, the
pigeons, and the dog.

The name tags, the pigeons, and the dog belong to a
recognized class of mystery, the parapsychological. The cryp-
tic tape is just a routine riddle of corporate intrigue. But as
Conrad insists, since ninety-nine percent of paranoia is justified, these mysteries have to be seen as a potential threat to
my welfare, if not to my very existence in the corporation.
Still, spending so much time worrying about them is debil-
itating. I have been worrying lately anyway about my physical condition. I have no appetite, and I am losing weight
rapidly. My sleep is disturbed. I wake up frequently, and
when I do sleep, it is a sleep of terrible nightmares, inhab-
ited by grotesque creatures oozing orange blood from a variety of inhuman orifices.

I report all of this to Dr. Mirsch, but he is unmoved.

"I'll be glad to prescribe something if you're having sleep
disturbance," he says blandly, swallowing a bite from a large
piece of chocolate cake.

"Forget it," I tell him. "I don't like to take pills. Besides,
I want to know what's happening to me. But I know better
than to expect answers from you."

10

THE SUPPLIERS SPEECH begins to take strange twists and turns. Since this is for the Chairman and because it is such an important speech, or so they say, we have started work on it even earlier than usual. We have gone through three drafts already, and none is deemed good enough to pass up to the Chairman. Barbara and Marlott have had at least two meetings with the Chairman. They give me his "thoughts" and provide me with tapes. Marlott has entered into this project with an unsual display of enthusiasm. He gives the impression that this speech alone will make or break him — and everyone involved in it.

We are writing the speech around Barbara's idea of "a formula for the future." A decent speech might have been written on the framework of this idea, but Marlott decides early on a gimmick that is certain to ruin it.

"Okay — here's what we do," Marlott tells Barbara and

me one day as he paces in front of his big corner window, great clouds of smoke pouring from his pipe. "We provide each supplier with a flagon and a set of vials. These are placed in front of each plate. As the Chairman reaches the point in the speech where he is about to discuss a new element in the formula for the future, he asks the suppliers to pour one of the vials into the flagon.

"For instance, when he comes to the element of new products, he asks them to pour the vial of green fluid into the flagon. When he talks about quality, he has them pour the red fluid into the flagon. Creative marketing might be the orange fluid. And so on.

"Now, obviously, the color of these chemicals has no direct relationship to the element discussed. That doesn't matter at all. But when the last vial is poured, *voilà!* The entire solution turns yellow — more properly, gold. And gold means money. Profits for the Company and profits for the suppliers who will share in the Company's prosperity!

"Well, what do you think of that? That ought to knock them off their seats!"

"Will it work, Mike?" Barbara asks.

Marlott looks slightly wounded.

"Of course it will work! Don't ask me how. I'm not a chemist. But I've already been in touch with our chief chemist and he says it can be done. It's just a question of identifying the right ingredients so that it all comes out gold in the end."

"Ah, Mike, won't these guys possibly spill some of this stuff?" I suggest. "I mean, it's a terrific idea and all, but there may be some accidents. We've got to be very careful how this thing is set up."

Marlott looks angry.

"There won't be any accidents because when the tables are set, everything will be in exactly the proper configuration.

It would take a spastic to have an accident with these things, and we don't have any spastic suppliers that I know of."

"Fair enough," I say. "But another thing we've got to guard against is toxicity. Somebody might get drunk and take a swallow out of one of the vials."

"You're being awfully negative. That's very far-fetched. Of course it won't be toxic, and besides, we aren't going to let anyone get that drunk."

"I think it's a highly original idea," Barbara says. "In fact, I think it's a smashing idea! It's visual, it's participative, and it's very upbeat. It is, in short, exactly what the Chairman ordered."

Marlott smiles his most generous smile.

"Great, Barbara! I couldn't have said it better myself. I love your positive attitude. You're right on the money, too, because the Chairman himself thinks it's a fantastic idea. He suggests we have a musical background of some kind — maybe something from *Fantasia,* like 'The Sorcerer's Apprentice.' We'll work out something. Now, let's get on with it!"

Since the first enthusiastic unveiling of Marlott's idea, the flagon plan has gone through several mutations. The Chairman keeps changing his mind about who should mix the chemicals and how. Apparently he has some of the same worries I have. First, he decides that a chemist should be seated at each table to mix the chemicals. Then he decides that he should don a laboratory smock and mix the chemicals himself. Finally, he decides that the chemicals will be mixed by the chief chemist, who will be stationed a few feet from the podium.

Every new plan necessitates revisions in the draft. In addition, the substance keeps changing as various experts in Marketing, Finance, Engineering, Legal, and other departments provide us with their "input" — an endless flow of additions, corrections, deletions, and new statistics.

We are now on the eighteenth draft, and the speech is only a week away. Someone — I have no idea who — has made a grievous error. Whoever it was reminded Marlott that the speech would be given on April Fool's Day, and when Marlott mentioned this to the Chairman, the Chairman clapped his hands together and said:

"We've got to end with a trick! Give me a trick. Let's end with something funny!"

Marlott orders people to put their heads together and come up with something funny. A committee is appointed and then broken down into subcommittees. The subcommittees are the outgrowth of a heated debate over what form the climax should take — an audio surprise, a visual surprise, perhaps a culinary surprise, such as a girl jumping out of a pie. Not exactly original, Marlott says, but worth considering.

"Leave no stone unturned," Marlott enthuses one day when he has gathered us all in his office. "Whoever comes up with the winning surprise wins a week's free trip to the Miami office. We'll put it down as 'research,' but there won't be any duties involved. A week's playtime in Miami in December!"

In the end, it is the Chairman who comes up with the winning idea. Marlott comes down from the Chairman's office one day with Barbara trailing behind, a slightly amused look on her face.

"That guy's a genius," Marlott declares. "Here's the game plan. The chemist mixes the solution. It comes up yellow — the color of gold. 'It's gold for all you suppliers!' the Chairman shouts. That's the final line of his speech. And then, sort of ad-libbing, the Chairman says that because it's April Fool's Day, the chemist is going to drink the concoction — actually drink it — with results guaranteed to surprise everyone!

"Then the chemist takes the flagon of yellow stuff behind a screen and pretends to be drinking it. And when he comes out from behind the screen, he's wearing a werewolf mask, a Reagan mask, or a Queen Elizabeth mask — whatever we can come up with that really moves us."

Marlott whirls around and punches a button on his intercom.

"Scarafini! This is Mike Marlott. Come on in here a minute."

Scarafini walks into the office breathing heavily. It is possible he has run all the way. Every department in every company has at least one Scarafini, someone with an obscure title who performs the familiar duties of the gofer. Typically, Scarafinis greet every assignment with enthusiasm, regardless of how trivial it is, how boring, or even how dangerous.

"Yassah, boss," Scarafini says, doing a little softshoe near the door. Scarafini is about fifty, and he has been with the Company since he graduated from high school. For him, the Company is everything — his livelihood, his social life, his hobby, his faith.

Scarafini is built like a boxer, and he is rumored to have killed a man who threatened the Chairman's life. Most of his time is spent procuring box seat tickets to sporting events for company executives and their friends, picking up cleaning and running other errands for top executives, and "sitting" with Marlott when no one else is available. He is paid a large salary, reportedly in the high seventies.

"Louie!" Marlott is beside himself with excitement. "Louie, this is a little off the beaten track, but you can handle it, I'm sure. What I want you to do is, I want you to go to some magic shop — toy shop or whatever — and pick up an assortment of masks — a werewolf mask, masks of monsters, Halloween masks, masks of real people. Get a whole assortment — fifteen or twenty — and get back here this afternoon so we can take a look at them."

"Yassah, Mr. Bossman," Scarafini replies, rushing out the

door. In return for his positive attitude, Scarafini is allowed to play the clown whenever he feels like it. He feels like it now, apparently, and Marlott only smiles.

"Quite a guy," Marlott says, letting us know the meeting is over. "Quite a guy."

11

As things turn out, Scarafini fails miserably at his urgent mission. The Chairman rejects all twelve of the masks he produces, claiming the whole batch shows no originality.

Marlott, furious, summons Scarafini and me in a high panic.

"If you guys don't produce something, and produce something the Chairman likes by the end of the day, I can kiss my career good-bye, and so can you," he shouts.

"I want you to pull out all the stops. I've put a chauffeur and a limousine at your disposal. Spare no expense. I want something original, something shocking, something that will grab the Chairman where it hurts. If you fail, you're finished, and I'm serious. If you succeed, there's a bonus in it for you. The Chairman is leaving for Florida at five o'clock this afternoon. I want his approval of it before he goes."

The big, extended limousine with the television, telephones, and bar in front of the rear seat hurtles down the freeway, driven by a madman. It is none other than Dominic Ferriano, a good friend of Scarafini's who chauffeured Scarafini on his ill-fated mission.

"I told you none of those was worth a damn," Ferriano yells at us, turning his head almost completely to the rear.

"Never mind, just drive," I shout.

The car pushes eighty-five as we sail down the freeway toward the center of town. The phone rings. It's Marlott, wanting to know how we are doing.

"We just got started, Mike," I say, "but we're making good time."

"Well, make better time. I want a report at every stop. If I'm not here, Stelritz will take the call."

"Yes, sir. Roger and out."

Scarafini busily attacks the bar. He pours himself half a tumbler of Chivas Regal and empties the glass in the time it takes us to turn onto a ramp and reach a surface street. Ferriano, who knows the city well, reaches our first destination in no more than three minutes. It's a dingy novelty shop on a narrow side street near the hotel district.

"Whatcha got in masks that's new and original?" Scarafini asks, taking hold.

The proprietor, a pale, fat man in his sixties with a sour mouth, goes to the back of the room and returns with an armful of masks. Wordlessly, he spreads them out on the counter and walks away.

The usual. Nixon, Agnew, Paul Newman, Hitler, a variety of animals and monsters, Marilyn Monroe, Humphrey Bogart, Donald Duck, Winston Churchill.

"Hey, what's this?" Scarafini yells to the proprietor, holding an unidentifiable mask against his face.

"Attila the Hun. Don't you recognize him?" the proprietor answers.

"A real joker," Scarafini says. "Let's get out of here."

The next stop proves equally fruitless, with a collection far smaller than our first store. And so it goes through the morning — a frenzied dash between magic stores, novelty stores, theatrical supply stores, toy stores.

"Let's get some lunch," Scarafini says just as the phone rings.

"How you coming?" asks Stelritz. I can hear his smile.

"Nothing yet. We were just about to break for lunch."

"Forget lunch," Stelritz replies. "We can't spare the time. Let me have a report on what you've got so far. I want stores visited, time spent in various establishments, an inventory of masks inspected, and any other pertinent information you want to give me. I'll expect your report by one o'clock."

I sign off as Scarafini pours himself another drink. He has had an amazing impact on the bottle, I notice.

Ferriano wheels the car toward our next stop, whistling some merry Neapolitan air. I use the time to scratch out some notes for the Stelritz report.

"Screw Stelritz," Scarafini mutters, reaching for more ice.

"What was the name of that last place?" I ask.

"I can't remember."

"Think. Stelritz will check."

"Tell him anything. What difference does it make? We're going to be fired, anyway."

We hit a pothole, and the car lurches sharply to the right. Ferriano struggles to regain control, but the car flies up over the curb, careens across the sidewalk, and smashes into a utility pole. We are shaken but unhurt. Ferriano leaps out of the car, trailing a string of untranslatable Italian. The hood has been lifted until it is almost vertical, and we hear glass spilling to the pavement.

I poke Scarafini with my elbow. "Put the drink down. Let's go."

"Go? What about the accident? What about the police?"

"Ferriano can handle it. Come on. They wouldn't want us to waste time."

"Christ." Scarafini groans, stumbling out of the car behind me.

At the next corner, I see a clock that says five minutes to one. Grabbing Scarafini by the arm, I rush into a drugstore and hurry to a phone in back. Stelritz himself answers.

"One o'clock on the dot," he says. "Report ready?"

I give him the report. We make up some names and fabricate a good half of the inventory, most of which we couldn't remember.

"Have you made any purchases?" Stelritz demands.

"No. Nothing worth buying ."

"I advise buying something. You can't come back empty-handed."

"Okay. Okay. Listen, we had a little mishap. Ferriano had an accident. We're on foot now."

"Never mind on foot. Take taxis. I'll get a back-up to you right away. Call in in half an hour and let me know the rendezvous point. And for God's sake, complete the mission."

Stelritz has lost his equanimity. I know that Marlott is putting on the pressure. I can visualize the whole scene, but I quickly put it out of my mind. The important thing now is to find something, anything, and convince them all that it is the perfect choice.

I almost lose Scarafini. Every store we hit has a bar nearby, and as I examine the merchandise, Scarafini disappears. I don't wait for him — just dash out of the store and hail the next taxi. Somehow, Scarafini's timing is perfect. He manages to order, drink, pay, and meet me outside in precisely the time it takes me to reject the latest mask collection.

At two-thirty, we rendezvous with the replacement limousine at a small park a few blocks from the river. Our new

driver is even more insane than Ferriano. We recognize him
as a former Public Relations driver who managed to run over
a reporter while showing off our new models at last year's
press preview.

At three o'clock, we have turned up nothing, and we have
exhausted the list of stores.

"Wait a minute," says Arnie, pulling the car to the curb
and pinching his nose just between his eyes, trying to remember something. "Yeah, I know a terrific place. It's in Dellville, but I can have you there in ten minutes. It's got the
biggest collection of masks you ever saw. I got my kid a couple for Halloween last year."

"What have we got to lose?" I say. "Let's go, Arnie."

Arnie floors the accelerator, and the tires scream. We take
off down a narrow side street, screech around corners, and
hit the freeway out of town. I think of the poor reporter, but
I don't care anymore. Scarafini has finished off the Chivas
Regal and is now attacking the Wild Turkey. The phone
rings for the fifth time this afternoon. It is Stelritz again.

I listen to his excited voice but can't make out what he's
saying. There's something wrong with the phone, and he
sounds as if he is speaking Japanese. Maybe he is. I hold the
earphone distractedly, idly gazing at the blur of tool and die
shops, warehouses, and discount stores that rushes by as the
city fades into the suburbs.

By the time Arnie reaches Dellville, I have hung up on
Stelritz — hung up without further ado, not saying a good-
bye, not offering apologies for the faulty connection.

Arnie pulls the car up in front of a large pink building of
concrete block. MONSTERLAND: COSTUMES, MASKS, MAGIC, TOYS
reads a badly painted sign above the door. Leaving Scarafini
asleep in the car, I rush inside.

The selection is truly phenomenal — more masks in one
store than we have seen all day. But my heart sinks. Most of

them are masks we have already seen and those that aren't
won't do.

The clerk, an enthusiastic young man with freckles, asks
me if he can help.

"Original, different, something new," I stutter, glancing at
my watch.

A quarter to four. It is now or never.

"Let's see," the clerk replies. "Wait a minute, I'll be back
in a minute."

When he returns, he is carrying a handful of masks. He
spreads them along the counter and I examine them quickly.
My heart leaps, because they are all masks I haven't seen
before.

Jesus. George Washington. Arnold Schwarzenegger. Mus-
solini, slightly shopworn. E.T. Judy Garland. Frankenstein.
Queen Elizabeth. Prince Philip. Chairman Mao. George
Bush. Debby Boone. Jiminy Cricket. Snoopy. Beethoven.
Pluto. Snow White. And others.

"All of these are ones I haven't seen before, but they won't
do," I say, my voice loud and almost breaking. "I need something scary. Very scary."

"Wait a minute," the clerk says, ducking beneath the
counter. I imagine he is playing some trick on me because
he stays hidden for a good two minutes. I can hear him shuffling faintly, opening and closing boxes.

Suddenly he emerges from the deep wearing a mask so
hideous that I reel backward. It is a mask of odd propor-
tions, a narrow face with a high forehead. The eyes are deep-
set, with tiny pupils of a strange orange cast surrounded by
whites crisscrossed with veins. The mouth is twisted in a grin
of murderous evil, revealing broken teeth that range from a
deep yellow to a dark brown. The long gray hair lies in a
solid mass, seemingly plastered with some heavy oil and
combed straight back against the scalp. The nostrils distend

ever so threateningly, and the ears rise to a narrow point like an animal's.

I step back and look out the window at the waiting car. The clerk laughs, a hideous laugh muffled by the mask.

"Who is that?" I manage to ask.

"That? Well, there's quite a story behind that." He laughs.

"Make it short. I'm in a hurry."

"Seems that a few months ago, there was going to be some big party of local richies — up north, at some fancy hunting lodge. Very exclusive. Only a few men, all millionaires. I mean the richest of the rich.

"Well, this guy comes in one day and gives me a photograph. 'Make me a mask in a hurry. I need it in two days,' he says. Well, we do that. We know a genius in New York who can knock these things out. But it costs. A lot. We charged him three thousand dollars, I think it was. We knew we could get it.

"Well, the day the guy was supposed to pick it up, he calls. I answer the phone, and a voice says, 'Forget the mask.' Well, God, I didn't recognize the voice. So I says, 'What mask?' And he says, 'The Mask of the Founder.' 'The who?' I says. 'The Founder, the very old man with the broken teeth.' Well then, see, I know who it was. I tell him okay, but the mask has already been made. I'd have to charge. He says fine, go ahead. And he paid it. Three thousand dollars."

"What was his name?"

"Markoff, something like that. A strange name."

"Marlott."

"That's it! Marlott. How'd you know?"

"I've heard of him. Wrap it up. How much do you want?"

"Well, it's been paid for once. Nobody else would want it, I guess. Give it to you for twenty dollars."

When I get back to the car, still shaking from the clerk's revelation, I can't believe what has happened. Arnie is nowhere to be seen, and Scarafini is sleeping, spread out on the back seat.

Angrily, I shake him.

"Where's Arnie?" I shout. "We've got to get going!"

"Oh, yeah, you won't believe this. He can't get the engine to start again. He went down the road to a gas station."

I rush back into the store. The clerk thrusts a phone at me and I dial Stelritz's number. It is four-fifteen. When Stelritz comes on the line, I outline the latest mishap. This time I have a good connection, and Mr. Efficiency comes through clearly.

"I'll send the helicopter," Stelritz shouts. "Where are you?" I give directions, hang up, and return to the car.

"What's doin'?" asks Scarafini, pouring himself a tall glass of gin.

"They're sending the helicopter."

"I can't believe it."

"Believe in all things."

The helicopter arrives within ten minutes, landing on a field beside the store. I pull Scarafini out of the car and we run over to it, climbing aboard under the whirring rotor. In seconds we are several hundred feet up, following the freeway back to headquarters. We arrive at four forty-five, take a vice-presidential elevator down from the roof, and rush down the corridor to Marlott's office.

"I don't know," Marlott says, gazing at the mask on Scarafini's face. "Who is it?"

"Don't know. Some rich man, I was told."

"Well, we'll try it out on the old man. Cross your fingers and say your prayers. It's scary enough, I'll admit that."

The following Monday, a beaming Marlott calls us in and informs us that the Chairman called him from Florida.

"You did it, you guys," Marlott says. "He loves it. He's crazy about it. You saved my job, your jobs, and earned yourselves a tidy bonus besides. Nice going. But there's one thing. He would like to know who it is."

"I'll get on that," I say. But I know I will never get the answer. Not for Marlott, anyway, who already knew. I could see him now at the party up north — the master fisherman become the master jester. A command performance before a rich and powerful audience. A little joke on the Founder, who couldn't be there. Good clean corporate fun. And now just another corporate mystery. The Mystery of the Founder's Mask.

12

THE NIGHTMARE resumes, and this time it lasts a week. I don't know what to call these new anomalies. It is as if I am lost in a carnival funhouse, unable to cry for help because I have lost my voice. Because in the atmosphere of the corporation, I know that to cry for help can create danger worse than any that exists in fantasies.

The first of the new sightings seems prosaic enough — a man standing behind Marlott's desk, his left hand on the edge of the chair, just standing there staring straight at me, a slight, half-quizzical smile frozen on his face for the minute or so I am in the room. He remains silent while I ask Marlott a brief question about the suppliers speech. Marlott spends that long minute writing on a memo pad, not looking up even when he finally gives me his curt, mumbled answer. The stranger is a heavyset Japanese, with thick glasses that almost completely conceal his eyes. I have never seen him before. In fact, I have never seen any Japanese in the building before. That is why his image is so clear and I remember his looks so vividly.

When I get back to the office, Marlott buzzes me with news of another speech to add to the schedule.

"Are you alone?" I ask.

"Yes."

"If you don't mind my asking, who was that Japanese man in there with you a couple of minutes ago?"

"What are you talking about? There wasn't anybody here. I've been alone all afternoon, except when you came in to see me."

"He was Japanese, kind of heavyset with thick glasses," I say. I am not going to be led astray by Marlott's habitual lying. "He was wearing a dark maroon tie and a navy blue suit."

"No such visitor here. Must have been someone else's office. Try to get more sleep. And don't be so nosy. I wouldn't tell you who it was even if someone had been here."

"No offense, Mike. I just thought possibly something important was happening with the Japanese."

Marlott clicks off. I know he is lying. But why? On the other hand, there is the very remote possibility that he is telling the truth. I think of the dog incident, and the still-unresolved question of the vanishing name tags. Was I seeing things? Taken separately, each of these incidents can easily be explained. But together they seem to form a pattern.

If nothing else had happened that week, I would have dismissed the appearance of the stranger as too trivial to worry about. But the very next day, something else occurs that forces me to conclude that things are seriously amiss. Either I am rapidly losing my grip on reality or certain people in the Company are trying to convince me I have.

It happens as I am walking down the long corridor to the cafeteria. Conrad is trying to beat a deadline, so I am having lunch alone. Suddenly, I hear a terrible scream, a piercing, high-pitched wail that echoes again and again as it seeks the end of the passageway. I stop, and my eye catches a fleeting image in the mirror at one of the corridor's abrupt turns — a glimpse of two uniformed men struggling with a young woman, pushing her back into a doorway. I hear the door slam loudly, and I make my way slowly around the corner, checking cautiously in both directions.

Nothing. The passageway is empty. I walk on, reading the signs on each of the doors, trying to tell which is the one that swallowed up the screaming woman and her two assailants. But there are no clues — just the obscure, meaningless labels I have puzzled over in the past.

At a door marked Room 111 — Latin American Operations and Planning — I stop. There is something about this spot — its distance from the mirror, perhaps — that makes me think this is the door I am looking for. I turn the knob and push. It is locked. I put my ear against the wood and listen. Silence. Then I hear footsteps coming down the hallway. I turn quickly and head for the cafeteria, my heart pounding.

The whole incident doesn't last more than two minutes, but an hour later, back in my office, I can't make the scene go away. Who was the screaming woman? Who were the men in the dark blue uniforms? Were they armed? Did anyone else, on the other side of the tunnel's bend, witness this scene? If they had, they must have disappeared quickly into one of the neighboring offices, because as soon as I rounded the bend, I was alone in the tunnel.

More grist for Dr. Mirsch's mill. It keeps him in cookies.

13

IT IS FRIDAY of the following week, and no new "sightings" have occurred recently. This has given me more time to think. Perhaps I ought to give myself up to Dr. Mirsch. He would be furious if he knew I was withholding all these events from him. Just as I am debating this, the intercom buzzes. It is Stelritz. He is involved with everyone in the department in one way or another, flitting from one office to another with stacks of papers and cheerful instructions. Conrad and I have assigned code names to certain key people so we can talk about them openly. What should we call Stelritz? He is a small man, with black hair combed straight back and perfect teeth that flash automatic smiles at the end of every sentence. Because he frequently volunteers for the hardest assignments and appears so delighted to expose himself to possible destruction, we have given him the code name Kamikaze.

"Can you drop over for a minute?" Kamikaze burbles into the intercom.

"Sure. See you in a second."

Stelritz's authority has never been formally declared, but he wears his power so lightly that none of us has ever thought to question it. His reputation is built on a terrible efficiency that meets every deadline, accepts every regulation without question, and settles for nothing less than perfection. He is the nearest thing to a corporate robot, but his usually efficient circuits occasionally emit an ominous, burning smell, as if they are overloaded.

As I walk to his office, I try to recall whether I once heard a rumor that Stelritz had, indeed, suffered a very human breakdown a few years ago, which put him in the hospital for several months. Possibly. Anyway, I know what he wants now. Marlott has decided that from now on, all speeches will be based upon a précis, a brief summary, no longer than a page, of the speech's content. Marlott is enthusiastic about the idea, believing it will give the whole speechwriting operation some class. He got the idea at a three-day public relations seminar in Phoenix, and a month or so later it was suggested by a thousand-dollar-a-day speech consultant who had breezed in for a three-day visit. The speech consultant spoke with great authority about the magical power of a précis in "systemizing the speechwriting function." This clinched it for Marlott, who called a meeting and announced that the procedure would be used starting immediately.

The whole thing had been a disaster. Far from "systemizing" the procedure, it only made it more chaotic. I recalled Conrad raging about it only a week after it had started.

"Did you ever hear of anything so idiotic? I mean, I can't believe it! The mind boggles, truly boggles. We write these goddamned things and they're nitpicked to pieces. Then we rewrite them and rewrite them again. Finally, they are approved, and by this time they are mere gibberish. But the gibberish is considered important. It's 'on the money.' Christ, if I hear that expression again, I'll kill myself. 'On target,' 'on stream,' 'on the money,' 'in the pipeline,' 'the bottom line' — all these expressions drive me nuts. Anyway, the gibberish gets Marlott's imprimatur. And you know what? That means we get to send it out for clearance. Copies of the goddamn précis go out to Marketing and Engineering and Finance and Legal — all over the goddamned place. Just like a speech draft. And then the whole process begins anew. Finance doesn't like this. Legal wants this changed. Engineering says add this. And all the copies of the précis come back. Marlott says make all the changes. What does he mean, anyway? Are you supposed to accept Legal's changes or Finance's or Marketing's? They conflict, they contradict each other. Doesn't the moron understand that? So it goes on and on. More drafts of the précis. The weeks go by. Nothing happens. The speech date gets closer, and we haven't even produced a first draft. It's outrageous! These people are fucking morons!"

"Calm yourself," I say. "Someone's going to hear you."

"I don't give a goddamn. This place is impossible."

Conrad is right. His raving is therapeutic, but it doesn't alter the situation a bit. There is no way of changing the procedure, either. One day, I summon up enough nerve to say something about it to Marlott.

"Mike, I just wonder, do you think this précis thing is really working?"

"What do you mean?" he asked, giving me his most threatening look.

"Well, it does create some problems. And I'm not sure the précis are all that useful."

"Look, let me remind you that you're getting paid for solving problems. The précis are recommended as highly constructive by the best minds in the business — thousand-dollar-a-day minds. So that's all I want to hear about it."

That settled the question. And now I am on my way to

Stelritz's office for another in an endless series of précis meetings.

As I enter the office, Barbara and Kamikaze are talking amiably. They stop abruptly, and Kamikaze switches to his normal mode of cheerful industry.

"Précis, précis, who's got the précis?" He chuckles. "Well, let's get going here." He looks down at a copy of my latest draft.

"Now when you say here 'the Company's future plans,' what time span are we talking about?"

"I'm not quite certain, Steve, because I haven't been told anything about these plans. So I just had to do some guessing."

"Well, it's tough to operate in the dark, isn't it? But I guess we've all got to fly on instruments around here sometimes. I'm going to change that to 'Company's prospective plans' and just cross my fingers that it gets through Finance."

"I think they'll buy it," Barbara says. "It's a bit more precise, and they do seem to like precision up there."

"And when you say 'economic indicators are improving,' what do you mean, exactly?"

"Well, things are getting better, that's what I mean. The statistics are looking better. I just talked to Finance yesterday about that."

"But consumer spending dropped last month." Kamikaze gives his flashing, about-to-dive smile.

"But that was the first month in ten. It's expected to climb again this month."

"Well, I think we'd better say, 'Generally, economic indicators are improving.' "

"Yes — that's a good change," I respond. The truth is, I have no opinion one way or another. It's as if we are playing bridge and I raise the bid from two to three hearts, hardly conscious of the game, my mind a thousand miles away.

I am learning how important it is to audit only certain situations, to avoid full participation. I am becoming increasingly skillful at reducing the level of outside stimuli while not losing the sense of the situation completely. Thus, while Barbara and Kamikaze drone on about small changes and additions, I concentrate on the pigeon incident and the other sightings. When questions are addressed to me, I am able to respond instantly, because I have reserved a fragment of my senses for the business of the meeting. If the others were leaping ahead with important conclusions and observations, I couldn't play my little game. But their movement is slow and the issues so trivial that one or two missed steps are not important.

Joining the discussion again after a short absence, I display heightened interest in order to offset any possible impression that I haven't been paying close attention.

The meeting is almost over. Kamikaze is beaming now, satisfied, as he says, that we have made "significant progress."

"There's light at the end of the tunnel," he says. "We'll have this précis finalized by the end of the week, and then we'll be ready to move into the first draft. I want to thank both of you for the great work you've been doing on this."

Barbara gets up to leave. I try to separate my dislike for her from my lust. Maybe they are closely related, I think. Maybe they depend on each other.

She brushes against me as she walks out. Was it an accident? No, I don't think so. Maybe the librarian is not so chaste and proper as she appears to be. Maybe someday I'll have a chance to find out.

It is less than an hour since the meeting in Kamikaze's office, and I have just about made all the changes to the latest précis draft. The intercom buzzes.

"Can you come in for a minute?" It is Marlott.

"Sure, be right there."

When I get to Marlott's office, he looks puzzled.

"You wanted to see me, Mike?"

"No."

"But didn't you buzz me?"

"No."

"Oh. Sorry. Maybe it was someone else."

Back in the office, I check the button. It is Marlott's and it is out, which means it was Marlott who buzzed me. Does this mean that I now have "hearings" as well as "sightings" to worry about?

The "hearings" and "sightings" are now augmented by a third phenomenon — absences. It is entirely possible that I have succeeded all too well in accomplishing what Conrad and I envisioned only as a joke — the psychic lobotomy. Boredom was the mother of invention. What has begun as an innocent enough flight from triviality has now escalated to a pathological state. It is one thing to tune out Barbara and Kamikaze while they dust the lint from a précis. It is entirely different to find that I have absented myself from whole blocks of time. What happened yesterday afternoon between one and five? Was there really a meeting of the sub-committee on social issues this morning? And what did Schwartz mean when he referred to the conversation we had yesterday in the men's room?

Absences. A frightening idea. Blackout at the OK Corral, with all the company gunfighters lying in wait for me. Presumably, I am able to conduct myself with a reasonable semblance of awareness and sanity during the periods when I excuse myself from the burden of consciousness. Are my eyes fully open during these periods? Is my speech slurred? Am I sweating heavily or twitching perhaps, like some idiot? A tic, hardly perceptible, would be fatal in this environment. The corporation raises consciousness of self, consciousness of others, far beyond natural limits. Books, newspaper columns, and seminars are devoted to describing proper corporate attire, how to behave in meetings, how to deal with superiors. And here I am, lapsing into oblivion for hours at a time. And that's not all. The thugs on the top floor are surely spreading the word that I had hallucinations about pigeons. Or Marlott himself may have told Barbara and others that I sometimes imagine hearing his voice over the intercom. All in all, I am naked to my enemies. Time to bring Dr. Mirsch up to date on what has been happening.

"What do I know about hallucinations?" Dr. Mirsch is really savoring his food today. I can hardly understand him, his mouth is so full. "What do *you* know about hallucinations?"

"Nothing. I've already told you about the pigeons, the dog, and the other things."

"Well, what are your thoughts?"

I am furious. He is getting seventy dollars an hour for asking me the same stupid questions. I lie silent for a while, hoping to convey my anger.

"Look — I don't have any thoughts," I almost shout finally. "Can't you tell me anything about this, why this is happening to me? Maybe these things are real. I believe they are real. And there's a chance — just a chance — that they are. Are these psychotic episodes? Have I crossed that thin line?"

"Maybe. Maybe not. Perhaps it would be helpful for me to say they are dreams. The entirely normal process of dreaming while you are asleep has been occurring during your waking hours."

"But what does it mean? Why am I encountering dogs and pigeons and hearing noises that aren't there and seeing people who aren't there? What's the significance?"

"We'll have to find out. The hallucinations — your term, not mine — are rooted in your subconscious. They have a definite link with incidents in your past — real or imagined incidents. These hallucinations are your own paintings, so to speak. I didn't paint them. You did. But we must not accept too literally the form and color of what we see on the surface. We must scrape that away and discover what lies underneath. If you dream of seeing a dog behind your desk, we must reach back and attempt to determine whether you saw that dog thirty years ago — whether you were frightened by that dog, or one just like it, or perhaps whether your family owned a dog like that, perhaps a dog that died or that you saw run over by a car.

"There are possibilities, you see, but we don't know for sure. We must explore. We are on a voyage of discovery together."

"Very poetic."

A long silence.

"Go on."

"Go on with what? Go on from where? What is the question before us? Where do we even start?"

And so the fifty minutes pass. A long freight train in the switching yard. Starting up. The groaning and the cranking noises. Stopping. Backing up. To the untrained eye and ear, switching without purpose. Is any progress being made? No need to ask. The answer is already there: "What do you think?"

"Tomorrow. We'll continue tomorrow."

14

KREIZNACH WANTS TO TALK to me about a draft, and I
have been summoned. Kreiznach is a director, one level below a vice president. Although he is in our department, I am
vague about his duties. His title is a small triumph of obfus-
cation: director of Communications Planning. You do not
ask a direct and pertinent question such as, "But what exactly do you do?" Observing Kreiznach on the rare occasions when I have been admitted to his sumptuous aerie, I
can only conclude that he doesn't do anything. But my superiors remark occasionally that he makes "a fantastic contribution" to the success of the department or, "We'd better
see what Kreiznach thinks about this." Kreiznach, then, is a
thinker, but the results of his deliberations are never revealed. You do not hear that Kreiznach disapproved of an
idea or had any opinion about it whatsoever. Nor do you ever
hear that an idea originated with Kreiznach. He is one of
many *éminences grises* who inhabit the headquarters build-

ing, presumably functioning in ways that are both powerful and secret. It is said that Kreiznach has the Founder's undying gratitude, the result of some heroic achievement years and years ago.

"Come in, come in." Kreiznach's smile is not one of the Harvard smiles; it is almost human. Rumor has it, in fact, that Kreiznach never went to college, one of those rare, nondegreed survivors of the Company's rambuctious early history.

"Sit down, sit down." Kreiznach always repeats everything, it seems. "Like a cup of coffee, care for some coffee? Listen, how about closing the door? There, thanks.

"I like the draft. I mean, I know it could be improved. But to hell with it. I don't feel like talking about it right now. Do you?"

"Whatever you want to do is fine with me, Charlie. It's up to you."

"Okay, let's listen to some more Wagner. Where were we last time?"

"Tristan und Isolde, Act One."

"Good, good. That's what I thought. You know, you've been under a lot of strain lately. I think this is just the thing for you. And for me, too."

He smiles his nearly human smile, but when I see it for the second time, I am less convinced it is real.

Kreiznach slips the tape into the player and the music pours into the office. He walks to the drapes and closes them, then sinks into his chair, putting his hands behind his head and closing his eyes.

The music plays on, and we say nothing to each other.

" '*Frisch weht der Wind, der Heimat zu: mein irisch Kind, wo weilest du?'*

"That means, 'The wind blows fresh toward my homeland. Where are you, my Irish child?' "

"Yes, that's nice," I murmur. Why did I say that, why do I

demean myself only to hold this stupid job? And what are we doing here listening to Wagner?

"Yes, it's a good draft. Needs work, though." His approval is waning. He is such a pleasant man. So pleasant, yet so threatening. Does he still talk to the Founder, that besotted survivor of indecent wealth who lives in a Xanadu somewhere south of Monterey? Do they swap stories about the old days before they all got rich, the days when cars were made to last and each family had only one in the garage? Do they gossip about the current management, plotting the elaborate re-alignments that are announced every few months, destroying dozens of careers and making dozens of others overnight?

"Here's where we get our first sight of Tristan," Kreiznach says. "A beautiful passage, if you like Wagner."

"Oh, I do, I do," I say. Kreiznach opens his eyes momentarily, then sinks deeper into the chair.

The music drones on. We are lazily making our way toward some coastline. I am getting sleepy, fighting to keep my eyes open and wondering what Kreiznach is up to. Not that this is a new experience. It is one of the few eccentricities known to exist in the huge building. That it is tolerated is further proof of Kreiznach's unique power.

Trumpets awaken me. Frantic, I pull myself up in my chair, hoping Kreiznach has not noticed. His eyes are still closed. I look at the digital clock on his desk. More than an hour has passed since I arrived, exactly on time. Is Kreiznach asleep? He could be, but my guess is that he is not. Without opening his eyes, without changing the position of his hands, he begins talking in a low voice, slightly ominous, less friendly than the voice he used when he greeted me an hour ago. I have trouble hearing him over the music.

"You know, you have been under considerable strain, I'm told."

That certainly demands an answer, a careful answer.

"Well, Charlie, I don't know who told you that. I've not been aware of it, frankly, but maybe it's showing up in my work."

He ignores this. The music brings a sudden smile to his face.

"They've taken the poison. They're supposed to fall dead, but they don't. This is a good part. Now get this. *'Wo bin ich? Leb' ich? Ha! welcher Trank?'* Did you get that?"

"Yes, sure." I lie. I can't make out any of it. "It's good, all right."

"It's almost over. Let's listen to the end. Just a couple of minutes."

The music ends. Kreiznach turns off the stereo and opens the drapes. He stands with his hands on the sill, gazing out the window.

"Good stuff, don't you think?"

"Yes, really beautiful. One of my favorites."

"We'll have to do the second act together."

Do the second act together? We are not appearing in an opera. Or are we? A curious and frightening man, Kreiznach.

"But in the meantime, we've got to deal with your problem."

My palms are beginning to sweat, but I know I should say nothing at this point.

"It is a problem we've been talking about for some time, some of us. And you know, we are not unsympathetic to you at all."

His voice becomes softer. I let him go on without interruption.

"In fact, the Company is very well organized to deal with such problems, because we realize that we're on a fast track and the pressures we are encountering are enormous, pressures that are felt by people throughout the Company."

"Yes." It is the first word I've spoken since he began. He

turns, sits down again, spreads his hands out on his desk, and lets his head sink down. His hands are clasped, prayerlike, and I notice for the first time that his fingernails are polished. His entire appearance is impeccable — a very expensive dark blue pinstripe suit, a tasteful striped tie, small but expensive cufflinks. Kreiznach pays a great deal of attention to his appearance, but the extreme care he takes is too apparent, a mistake not made by younger men in the Company.

"So we are sympathetic, and we are anxious to help. The committee has discussed your case and we've come to a decision. We would like you to consult with our Troubled Employee Department."

"I didn't know there was such a department."

"Oh, yes. Not many people know about it because, quite frankly, we don't have many troubled employees. Now I certainly don't want you to think that any stigma attaches to this decision. In fact, our policy is that your personnel records will never in any way reflect that you were referred to the department in question. And when I mentioned the committee, I did not mean to suggest a large number of people. There are, in fact, only three, each of them highly placed in the corporation and each of them accustomed to handling this kind of problem with the utmost discretion."

Kreiznach reaches over for a memo pad and begins writing. I know that the interview is over.

"Now," he says, not looking up, "let me offer just a couple of suggestions to make this all go smoothly. Number one, please don't talk about this to anyone, not even your very good friend Conrad."

"Right, Charlie."

"And two, don't let this affect your work. Your work has been entirely satisfactory. I know that something like this can affect your self-confidence, and self-confidence is as important to a writer as a hammer is to a carpenter. So go into it with the right spirit. The corporation is trying to help you. The corporation has extremely valuable experience in this field and the most highly qualified practitioners in the country to advise it. They are experts in their field, and on top of that they are all very fine people, very warm and human. They've been alerted to expect you. They are familiar only with the bare bones of your case — the hallucinations and the events in Los Angeles — but they will expect you to co-operate fully by telling them everything you know. You must tell them when your troubles first began, and you must tell them all you remember about the trip to the coast. Let me emphasize that this will all be treated with the utmost confidentiality. Your speech, and all the work that you have pending, will be reassigned. People don't usually get nosy about what others are doing in the Company, and that's a good thing. But in case anyone asks when you return to duty, you are to say simply that you were on temporary assignment in Finance. Any questions?"

"How long will this, ah, treatment last?"

"Two weeks at the outside. But I should think, because I know that you are basically strong and stable, I should think you could wrap it up in even less if you just give it your best effort, relax, and let the treatment work."

Kreiznach looks up at me with his most pleasant smile, and once again, I am convinced that he is one of the few human survivors of the old guard who set the Company in motion more than four decades ago.

"Anything else you want to know?" Kreiznach asks.

"Where do I go?"

"Oh, yes. That is kind of important, isn't it? The basement, Room 111."

"And when?"

"Right now, if you don't mind."

If I don't mind, indeed. You are not allowed to mind.

Well, you are allowed to mind, but you are not permitted to show it.

Kreiznach emerges from behind the desk and shakes my hand warmly. Now I feel the presence of an authentic human being. Except for meeting Conrad, it is the first such experience I can recall since I arrived at the corporation seven years ago. I feel good about everything — about the music, about my job, about Kreiznach, even about Marlott.

"Thanks a lot, Charlie, thanks for your help. I really appreciate it."

"That's all right. Don't mention it. There are one or two other things I should mention. The first is that I would not be sending you to the department if I didn't believe it would help you. And I certainly believe that because I went through the experience myself, many years ago.

"Oh, I know, many people believe the corporation is all business, without any regard for the personal welfare of the employee. But that is a bunch of crap. This program is good, it works. I know that not only because I'm a graduate, but also because I helped design it.

"The second thing is that before you report down there, you should call anyone who will miss you and let them know you will be gone for a few days. Tell them two weeks. Tell them you are going out of the country on company business or something. There won't be an opportunity for you to call anyone while you're in the program, so be sure to do it now. Do you understand all that?"

"Yes, of course. Well," I say, trembling as I stand, "let me say again how helpful you've been, Charlie. Let's get together when this is all over and listen to the second act."

"You're on."

Charlie goes back to his desk and I find myself in the corridor, dazed but competent enough to make my way back to the office. When I have finished making my calls, I sit staring out the window. Troubled Employee Department? I've never heard of it. And out of touch for two weeks? This is all ridiculous. My first impulse is to call Conrad and demand an immediate debriefing. But I think better of it. Charlie told me not to talk to anyone about this, and I had better follow his instructions. Second, how did they know about the hallucinations? Nobody knew but Conrad. Conrad alone. Oh, yes, and Dr. Mirsch.

Yes, as Conrad likes to say, ninety-nine percent of paranoia is justified.

15

ROOM 111 FULFILLS my worst fears. It is, of course, the same room in the long basement corridor where the thugs had pushed the screaming woman not so long ago. Now I find myself turning its polished brass doorknob and opening a door made even more forbidding by its obscure label, Latin American Operations and Planning.

The opulence of Room 111, or the reception area, anyway, exceeds the opulence of the vice-presidential offices on the thirty-second floor. There is more marble, the carpets are deeper, the original paintings more impressive, the receptionist's walnut desk even larger. Are the occupants more important than the vice presidents themselves?

"Come in, sit down, we were expecting you," says the blond receptionist. "Dr. Mangones will be with you in a minute. Please relax and don't worry. You may smoke if you like, and there are magazines to read."

She could have been delivering a memorized statement. Her voice was perfectly even, without inflection, the look on her face the look of someone drugged. Perhaps she has been, I think.

A buzz breaks the silence. "Yes, Dr. Mangones, he's here. Shall I send him in? You may go in now, sir."

Dr. Mangones' office is sanitized splendor, a kind of operating room with couches and carpeting. None of these offices has windows. The Troubled Employee Department evidently occupies the very center of the building. Perhaps the thinking is that windows are distracting, especially to troubled employees.

"Have a seat, yes, have a seat," Dr. Mangones says in a voice that is hardly louder than a whisper. I sink into a chair placed directly in front of him, only a foot or two from his desk.

"Care for a cigarette? Would you like a cigarette?" Is it possible that Dr. Mangones has the same echospeak habit as Kreiznach? "Or perhaps something to drink, a little drink. You know, we are more relaxed down here than people in other parts of the Company, and we would like our clients to be, too."

No, I tell him, I don't smoke and I don't want a drink, thanks very much.

"Well, let us proceed," Dr. Mangones says in a voice that is even softer than at first.

"You see, we have read your files and viewed your videotapes, a preliminary to our first interview with each of our clients. We take the view that there is nothing 'wrong' with you, 'wrong' in the sense that this word is customarily used. Of course, as you might imagine, we believe ourselves that the title of our branch, the so-called Troubled Employee Department, is something of a misnomer. That is to say, we do not believe that our clients are 'troubled' in the sense in which that word is usually employed."

Dr. Mangones inhales deeply, blowing the smoke carefully downward. A thoughtful and sensitive man, I think.

"No, not troubled. But, as the files and the recordings would tend to indicate, 'different.' And while I don't like to keep fine-tuning these phrases, even the word 'different' is somewhat misleading, because it implies a variation from the normal style, outlook, opinion, and behavior of the great mass of people whom one might encounter in the so-called outside world. No, that is not what we're after here. We are not attempting to define the ways in which your conduct, attitude, and behavior might be at variance with those of the so-called average person. Nor is it simply a matter of pointing out to you how it might differ from those of the so-called average executive in a large corporation."

Dr. Mangones pauses again, this time to blow his nose. Whatever kind of man he is, he is not overburdened with "clients." He is taking his time, apparently trying to put me at ease.

Suddenly it dawns on me why he looks familiar. He is the man with the pointer behind the drawn curtains at Marlott's house so long ago. It all becomes clear; it was he who had made the videotapes of my performance in meetings and provided the critique for Marlott.

"No, it is not the 'average' corporate employee who serves as our standard here," he continues. "It is the 'average' employee of our own corporation who defines the optimal behavior and attitude. As you must understand, the idea that all corporations are pretty much the same is an unfortunate myth perpetrated by the media, which must always find simple ways to explain these things.

"In reality, every corporation has a distinct personality, marked by subtle yet important variations that are not recognizable to the untrained eye.

"Now, a question that immediately occurs to each of our clients is why the corporation must strive to achieve uniformity among its employees, especially among those who occupy sensitive executive positions such as yours. That is a very sensible and important question, of course.

"And the answer is that each employee, in order to serve best the interests of the corporation, must adopt in every aspect of his appearance, attitude, and conduct the so-called persona of the corporation itself.

"When one stops to think about this concept, one realizes that it is marked by a compelling and perfect logic. For the corporation is far more than the building that its headquarters staff occupies. It is the sum of thousands of individual personalities, each of them carefully adjusted, sculpted, and shaped, as it were, in the likeness of the corporation."

Dr. Mangones pauses again, but this time for no apparent reason. He stares at me with the look of an inquisitor who has demanded to know my whereabouts on the night of a certain mass murder or the location of a whole division of my army. It is a look that says there is no doubt that I shall respond, quickly and truthfully.

"Yes, I see what you're driving at."

Dr. Mangones ignores my somewhat unimaginative response.

"To continue," he says, and there is a faint note of annoyance in his voice. "To continue. The parameters of personality that we seek to establish are not those of appearance alone, because those are easily established, and, in the corporate environment, adopted almost without question by almost all employees.

"No, we concern ourselves here with what one says when he speaks, and, of course, how he says it. Not how he says it in terms of language alone, but how he says it in terms of what is equally important — nonverbal language. Please remember as I am speaking that while I use the male first-person pronoun, I am talking about female employees as well. My use of the male pronoun is for convenience only.

"Now it is not my purpose here to explicate every example of your personality that fails to meet the corporate norm. But to give only one example — a small example, you might think — you have been observed from time to time walking with a rather slouched and depressed style, especially when you are on your way to meet with one of your superiors." Dr. Mangones is turning the pages of a file.

"That in itself may seem to you a trivial deviance. And indeed it is, when examined only on the surface. But when one considers this style of walking as an attitudinal symptom, one is forced to the conclusion that you are either depressed or, I hate to use this word, uncooperative or even hostile. Do you begin to see what I mean, what I am driving at?"

"Yes, of course, yes." I am quickly acquiring the habit of echospeak. I straighten myself in my chair and look more directly into Dr. Mangones' eyes. I smile the faint hint of a smile that I have observed in so many of my colleagues. Perhaps this would not be so difficult, after all.

"So without further explication" — it is one of Dr. Mangones' favorite words — "let me give you a brief rundown of the treatment program.

"First, some reassuring words. There is nothing arduous or unpleasant or even in the least embarrassing about the treatment you will receive here. Once again, I hesitate to use the word 'treatment'; a more accurate word would be 'conditioning,' perhaps. Yes, let's say 'conditioning.'

"No. Emphatically no. There is nothing unpleasant about the conditioning you will receive in the next two weeks. Briefly, the program is broken down into four phases, including a number of subphases.

"The first phase — and let me say once again that I am not altogether happy with the words used to describe these phases — is called Positive Attitudinal Reinforcement, or PAR, as we on the staff commonly refer to it. The second part of the program is known as Extra-corporate Environment Norms, or EEN. The third is designated Supervisory Aptitude Development, or SAD, and the fourth, Management Adaptability Seminar, or MAS.

"I imagine that you are quite anxious to hear some explication of what will occur as you enter these various phases of the program, but we have found over the years that deviants — I mean to say clients — should not be informed about the nature of the conditioning that occurs. The surprise element greatly enhances the results of our training efforts." Dr. Mangones' smile is slightly ominous. "So. Are there any questions?"

I don't have time to answer before he answers for me.

"No questions. Good. Then we will proceed. From here, you will be escorted to your quarters for the next two weeks. I assume you have informed members of your family that you will not be returning home every night."

I notice for the first time that Dr. Mangones' voice has the slightest trace of an accent.

"Good. Well, then, you will be escorted to your quarters, and I am confident that you will find them more than adequate. For the rest of this day, you are perfectly free to do what you want. Of course, you must remain in your quarters. You will use the time to read, watch the television, listen to music, or just contemplate. I might suggest, if I may, that contemplation might be the most useful purpose to which you can put this time. After all, you may have some ideas yourself about how your personality might be altered to fit more closely the corporate norms. Your ideas will be given close attention. You must remember that this program is entirely cooperative. And you should keep in mind throughout the period of training that the corporation has nothing but your best interests in mind.

"Well, then" — Dr. Mangones smiles a smile that is genuinely friendly — "let's get on with it." He stands up abruptly, reaches under his desk, and appears to press a button. Then he reaches over the desk and extends his hand, a hand that is large and rough, with a grip that is painful.

"I want to wish you the best of luck. My initial impression is that you will be a most successful graduate of our program. I can see through various signs that would not be evident to you that you are, basically, a cooperative and even compliant person. I know that the training you receive during the next two weeks will be of immense importance to you personally and to the corporation as a whole."

It is a nice little speech, but I feel a chill run through my body. The door I entered a few minutes ago opens and a young man in one of the trainers' uniforms enters.

"Yes, Dr. Mangones?"

"Please escort this man to his quarters immediately."

"Yes, Dr. Mangones. Come with me, please."

16

My "QUARTERS" leave nothing to be desired. Why are these people so accommodating? Everything has been done with taste and care, from the oak-paneled walls to the large-screen television to the well-stocked bookshelf. Well-stocked, yes, but on closer inspection I find that the selection is strictly corporate conservative. The complete works of Ayn Rand. The complete works of William F. Buckley, Edmund Burke, various memoirs and commentaries of Richard Nixon, and so forth. I have my own refrigerator, my own bar. I switch on the television and pour myself a double Scotch. I sink into a leather couch and stare dumbly at the evening news, not hearing what is said or absorbing what I see. I am worried, afraid. It is all too pleasant, all too comfortable. I continue drinking for a couple of hours, then take a shower and climb into bed. I know it is early, but I am exhausted. Still, I can't sleep. I lie there thinking about what a strange place a corporation is.

Dr. Mangones told me to use this period for contemplation. About what? Perhaps about the corporation. Why I am here in the first place and why I don't fit in. I try to explain this to people. What is there about it that I dislike so much? Answer: everything, except the money.

I think about being back in the office and being visited by Charlie Corman, one of the men in Personnel. Charlie came to apologize for the long delay in getting my paintings framed. He assured me that they would be up on my walls within a week. He fidgeted, smiled a lot, and seemed very anxious that I not take offense because the paintings had been in the Graphics Department for five months. I tried to reassure him.

"Look, Charlie. It's okay. It's okay. Without you, nothing would have happened. I'm just grateful that you were able to accomplish something. But let me ask you one thing. In all candor, doesn't the delay have something to do with the fact that someone in my classification doesn't qualify to have paintings on his wall?"

Charlie squirmed and looked at his watch. "Well, they have been awful busy down in Graphics. They just weren't able to get around to it yet."

"Come on, Charlie. It was the classification thing, wasn't it? My level was not high enough to qualify. Isn't that right? What it boils down to is that I'm not considered important enough to have paintings on my walls. Right?"

Charlie's head drifted back and forth in embarrassment.

"Well, ah, you're right," he said, "but I wouldn't put it that way myself. Anyway, I took care of the problem. So not to worry. Nobody's going to say a thing. It's just one of those company rules. I mean, there's probably a good reason for it. There probably just aren't enough paintings to go around."

The paintings were original watercolors commissioned for covers of one of the Company's publications. The friendly woman in charge of the storeroom where they were kept had asked me if I would like to borrow some for my office walls, which were white and bare, giving the effect of a prison cell.

I was delighted. They were good paintings, and I picked out three I liked.

It was something of a mystery why the people in Graphics approached the problem the way they did. Perhaps they were too embarrassed to tell me that my lowly classification made me ineligible to borrow the paintings. More likely, they were reluctant to reveal that the question was a matter of company policy.

But the question of who qualifies to hang paintings on his walls is, indeed, very much a matter of company policy, part of an exhaustive, complex, but precise system of law that covers a thousand rights and privileges from travel on company business to office furnishings. All of this is spelled out in a company manual, I am told, but I have never seen the manual and do not know anyone who admits to having one.

Still, it is very clear that this mysterious guide sets forth an elaborate table of employee worth. Depending on their rank, employees are entitled to offices of varying size, from the huge corner offices of the kind occupied by Marlott down to tiny cubicles with no windows at all. I have a two-window office, which is about in the middle of the scale. The size of the office is only the beginning of a system that is as intricate as ranks in the German army. High-level employees qualify for Venetian blinds and drapes; lower-level employees have to adjust the light with shades. A water carafe and cups are assigned to employees of a certain rank and above. Employees of certain lower rankings have desks of plastic and steel, while those of higher station have desks of oak or walnut. The number of chairs in one's office is a clear sign of grade, just like the number of windows. Some of the steerage-class employees are apparently not expected to have visitors at all, because the only chair they are entitled to is the one behind their desks. A

Hold button on a telephone is available only for employees above a certain level, the thought apparently being that lower-ranking employees would not be likely to receive more than one call at a time. A credenza behind the desk to hold books and other items is one of the more important perquisites of the higher ranks. And one of the most prized badges of station is the company car. Even these are allotted in accordance with rank and station. The directors and vice presidents, the corporate equivalents of dukes and barons, are given a new car every three months, free gasoline, and a reserved parking place in the underground structure. Every day, attendants check the cars of the nobility, fill the gas tanks, look for mechanical problems, wash them, and return them to their reserved places. A great number of lower-ranking employees are also assigned company cars, but they must buy their own gasoline and provide maintenance. Further down the line, a class of employees is allowed to lease cars at a very low rate, even two if they are of a certain grade. The company lawyers deny that the free cars are a form of income subject to taxation. They maintain that all the thousands of employees given car privileges are actually testing the vehicles.

It is hard to escape the class structure, even at lunch. Since the building is so isolated, few people can take the time to eat outside. The various places where employees are authorized to eat are assigned on the basis of rank. The vice-presidential dining room would easily rate four stars in any guide of the Company's eating establishments, with its luxurious surroundings and its exhaustive menu, first-rate service, and superb food. Several hundred executives are entitled to eat in the less luxurious executive dining room. Beneath them is another class of employees, from junior accountants to secretaries, who are permitted to eat in one of two cafeterias.

Long-term employees, or those who have experience in the Personnel Department, are often highly skilled at determining an employee's classification from the perquisites he enjoys. They can glance inside an office and tell in an instant whether the occupant is a grade nine or ten, and so forth. Perquisites are assigned in kits or packages. Thus, it is not possible to have three chairs and no water carafe. The three chairs, water carafe, credenza, and other essential items are all of a piece, so to speak. Just as a king would be considered an impostor with only a crown and not a scepter, so, too, would a manager be considered a charlatan if any part of his official package of perquisites was not found in its proper place.

When Harry Egret, who had been assigned to Personnel a number of years before and was an expert on these things, walked into my office one day, his face took on an expression of alarm.

"Where's your carafe?" he demanded.

"Oh, I never use it. I keep it in the credenza."

"You have the three glasses?"

"Oh, sure."

He seemed satisfied with this.

Not all employees have learned the perquisite system, and so while they might have some idea of a colleague's grade, they can't be certain by any means. This can lead to embarrassing situations. Once, after I had been here only a few months, someone invited me to meet him for lunch in the executive dining room. I had to explain that I wasn't qualified to eat there. He apologized and added that we would go to a restaurant outside the building sometime. But he never got around to asking me again. Of course, he could have joined me in the cafeteria that day, but as time went by, I saw that this was rarely done — the public mixing of ranks far apart.

In fact, as I later learned, one might assume that those employees who socialized together were exactly the same classification, or within only one or two grades of each other.

There was a clear effort among many of my colleagues to be seen with those of higher grades, but those of lower rank were avoided, except where the business of the office demanded contact.

Supporting this elaborate class system does not put any real stress on the Company's resources. The system may cost a few million dollars, but since the Company earns several billion dollars a year, the cost is insignificant. Still, assuring that everyone gets exactly the perquisites he is entitled to, no more and no less, requires close and continuous attention by a large number of personnel people. Maintenance crews are also kept busy moving furniture in and out of offices as people get promoted or reassigned.

For example, a man was promoted to director and transferred from another building to ours. When he arrived, he set about measuring his new office and found that it was four inches narrower than it was supposed to be. Maintenance men were summoned immediately and corrected the situation by moving one of his walls out four inches. This was not as hard as it sounds, because the building's architects, apparently told about the importance of hierarchical trappings, installed walls that could be moved simply by removing a few brackets. In the case of the newly promoted director, moving the wall four inches took only a few minutes. But it started a chain reaction that required a dozen walls to be moved up and down the hallway so that the occupants of those offices would end up with the proper amount of space. When all the walls were in place, the maintenance men found that a four-inch gap had been created between two offices. But they decided the gap could not be eliminated without giving someone an office that was four inches too wide. So it was left intact.

Authorized perquisites are only one part of the Company's class system. Higher-ranking officials enjoy many unofficial favors that are not widely known and appear in no record books. In certain cities, the Company maintains suites in luxurious hotels that are always at the disposal of the highest executives, whether on private or public business. Company airplanes ferry the highest executives back and forth between headquarters and their winter homes in Florida or Palm Springs and on hunting trips to Canada. One story is that a top company officer was regularly flown to New York in a company jet just to get a haircut from his barber of many years. Another story is that a high executive had a company jet make an unscheduled landing just to pick up a pack of cigarettes for his girlfriend.

High-ranking executives such as vice presidents or directors often call upon subordinates, secretaries, and lesser employees for favors. Secretaries go shopping for their bosses as a matter of course, type school papers for their children, and perform a wide variety of personal favors. Other functionaries chauffeur the wives of top executives on shopping trips or to and from luncheons. They are also called upon to do carpentry, wiring, and plumbing, run errands, and perform a variety of other tasks according to their skills. One lesser executive has built his career on his expertise in the stock market. He spends most of his time on the phone to brokers and on his computer, handling stock transactions for his boss.

The extent of these perquisites — how much they cost the Company and how much of the employees' time they consume — is never discussed, of course, even though the Company prides itself on its efficiency and hundreds of people are assigned to figure out ways to cut a few pennies from the cost of one of its products. Once in a while, a stockholder hears about some extraordinary abuse of an executive's privileges and makes an issue of it at the annual meeting. But these questions are always skillfully deflected by the Company's general counsel, who has prepared for them with a flood of facts and figures that prove nothing improper has taken place.

All in all, the privileges enjoyed by high-ranking employees are considered very important, for their monetary value, their convenience, and their worth as status symbols. I have never heard of anyone refusing to accept the perquisites he is entitled to. And even if an employee asks to have only three chairs instead of the four he is due, the request is denied. Rank in our Company has many privileges, and they are mandatory.

My thoughts about these perquisites are interrupted by a loud voice that seems to come from every part of the room. I sit up in bed abruptly, realizing only then that I have drifted off to sleep.

"You are fortunate to be here. I advise you to get a good night's sleep and not be overly concerned about the nature of the training you will begin tomorrow."

The voice is familiar and loud. Startled, I sit up and look around the room.

"Don't be alarmed. We are simply making one of our precautionary observations. Go back to sleep and have a good night's rest. We shall be conferring again tomorrow."

It is Dr. Mangones, his face stretched across the giant TV screen, his voice filling the room. My heart starts pounding rapidly and my palms begin to sweat. I remember that I have turned the TV volume off, which means that someone has been in the room during my brief nap. It's obvious, too, that someone has been watching me, perhaps Dr. Mangones himself. I know now that the comfortable suite with its enormous bathroom and excessively stocked bar offers no more privacy and no more freedom than a prison cell. I pour myself another drink, then another. Self-consciousness overcomes me, because I realize that my every move is being watched. I jump up from the couch and move frantically around the room, determined to smash the hidden eye that is focused on me.

But I find nothing that resembles a TV camera — not the smallest opening in a wall, not anything suspicious behind the abstract paintings. More exhausted than before, I plunge back into bed and pull the covers over my head like a frightened child.

This is all beyond belief — a luxurious penal colony operating in the very heart of corporate headquarters. If only I can sleep, I may be able to face what will happen in the morning with reasonable calm. I am being fed and sheltered, after all, and there is no reason to believe that my warders are not trying to help me. But what a strange kind of help they are providing, the oppressive "help" of a huge and powerful organization determined that its employees will be as uniform as its products.

17

I MUST HAVE FALLEN back to sleep finally, because I am awakened by a soft knock on the door. Without waiting for me to answer, a uniformed "technician" enters, carrying a large breakfast tray. He sets the tray on the desk, turns with a smile, and says, "Enjoy your breakfast, sir. The first training session begins at seven-thirty sharp. That's a half hour from now. A technician will arrive then to escort you to the Trainorium."

The breakfast is hearty — eggs, bacon, potatoes — a breakfast designed for someone about to do physical labor, not someone who is to receive instruction in something called Positive Attitudinal Reinforcement. I eat quickly because I want time for a shower, but I barely have my clothes on when there is another knock on the door and yet another technician enters without my invitation.

"Please follow me, sir. I will take you to the Trainorium."

This technician is not as pleasant as the one who woke me

up, and he walks so fast I can hardly keep up with him down
the long green corridors that lead to the Trainorium. He opens
the door and leads me into a large room that resembles a gym.
The first thing that strikes me is the harshness of the light,
a light whiter and more brilliant than I have ever seen before. The light and the room's silence make me feel that I've
walked into one of those severely modern churches whose
priests play the guitar and whose congregation must greet
each other with a kiss. But this church does not have the
advantage of stained glass windows, or of any windows, for
that matter. Further, there are no pews, no furniture at all
except a large number of gleaming chrome and leather exercise machines and some very expensive-looking and garishly
colored mats on the floor. Suddenly I realize that my escort
has disappeared and that I am alone in the room. Then I
notice that the room is not altogether silent, but filled with
music. Wagner: "Forest Murmurs" from *Siegfried*. A voice
interrupts the music.

"Please be seated on one of the mats." I do as I am told.

A door opens at the far end of the room and a technician
enters. He is a giant, with only short gray stubble on the top
of his huge head and a face that is deeply tanned, scarred,
and weathered. He walks toward me quickly, his face un-
smiling.

"I am Carl, your physical conditioning technician," he begins in a voice from a late night World War Two movie, the
voice of an SS Obergruppenfuehrer. "I am a member of Ak-
tiongruppe, that is, Action Group Number One, which has
been assigned to your case. We have no time to lose, so do as
I say and don't ask stupid questions. Now, go to Machine
Number One."

I jump up and walk toward one of the gleaming exercise
machines with a sign that identifies it as Number 1. It resembles a weight-lifting bench, with a jumble of cables,
weights, and gears.

"Lie down and relax," Carl commands.

Again, I do as I am told. The bright metal is cold and the leather hard and soiled, as if by sweat.

"Stretch your arms out behind your head as far as you can," Carl grunts. He fastens straps around my wrists and secures my legs to the end of the bench with steel straps. I have never before been on an exercise machine like this, I think, and it is not comfortable. Perhaps it represents some new weight control and muscle toning technique.

"Now," Carl says, "we are about to begin. At first, you will experience some discomfort, but that will disappear as treatment continues. It will disappear, however, only if you adopt the Right Mental Attitude — what we call RMA — during the course of the treatment. RMA is perhaps the most important component of the PAR part of your training. What does PAR stand for?"

Just as I am about to answer, the machine jerks violently and a piercing pain surges through the entire length of my body. I writhe around, trying to see Carl. But he has disappeared.

"For Christ's sake, stop it!" I scream. The stretching eases up and the pain diminishes. I hear Carl's voice again, this time over the loudspeaker.

"Do not make unauthorized comments. You will speak only in answer to questions. Now, once more, what does PAR stand for?"

"Positive Attitudinal Reinforcement!" I shout.

"Correct." Carl increases the pulling pressure and the pain intensifies. As he does this, the voice of Dr. Mangones comes over the loudspeaker.

"In spite of your unauthorized outburst, you have made a positive beginning," Dr. Mangones says. "Now, you might logically inquire, if you were permitted to inquire at all, why we are causing you this degree of pain. The answer is quite simple. We have found through our studies of prisoners of

war in various conflicts throughout world history that pre-
conditioning to pain is a vital help in raising one's capacity
for suffering in silence, whether the discomfort is physical or
mental. It is as simple as that. Further, we have found
through our own studies here in the department that the ability to withstand physical suffering dramatically increases the
capacity for enduring mental anguish. The correlation is direct and clear.

"Obviously, in the corporate environment, you will not experience the kind of pain you will have to endure during this
conditioning process. But you will find that the experience
will greatly increase your capacity to withstand the kinds of
mental anguish, harassment, criticism, and humiliation that
are an unfortunate but essential part of corporate life.

"Your first session on Machine Number One will last ap-
proximately three hours. When it is over, you will be given
lunch, a half hour's rest, and then returned to the Trainorium for the afternoon session. Good luck, and happy conditioning!"

Dr. Mangones' voice stops and the Wagner resumes. This
time it's "Siegfried's Rhine Journey," played on a scratchy
record that must have been made in the thirties. The pulling
increases almost imperceptibly, and the pain intensifies. Minutes, hours, pass, and I am bathed in sweat. I shout and
scream, but the music goes on and there is no relief. The pain
becomes me, and the pain becomes the machine. Then the
room itself becomes a great, searing weight that closes in on
me, making my body smaller and smaller until I am only the
size of an insect, crushed on a huge expanse of concrete by a
giant heel. The heel turns orange, then purple, red, and
green, and finally black. The music almost fades out completely, and I imagine I am drowning. Just as I am about to
lose consciousness, the stretching stops abruptly, and a voice,
deep and soothing, blares from the loudspeaker.

"The forces of the free market are the nation's salvation."
Then, after a second or two, "Loyalty to the Company is the
greatest of all virtues."

Then the stretching resumes abruptly, more wrenching
than before. I sink into unconsciousness.

Dimly, as if dreaming, I am aware of being unstrapped. I
hear Carl's gruff voice and feel his damp and putrid breath
against my face as he works with the buckles.

"Not good. You did not do so good. Now you will eat."

Carl pushes me out the door of the Trainorium. I stumble
in the corridor and am about to fall when he catches me and
shoves me along.

"Move, we have no time to lose."

Lunch is served in a small room with Spartan furnishings.
Carl, doubling as a waiter, brings me a bowl of thin, luke-
warm gruel with a few crackers and a glass of water. I taste
one of the crackers. It is damp and stale. I stir the soup dream-
ily, but it contains no substance. Once more, I lose consciousness and awake to find myself stumbling along in the Trainorium, urged on by Carl's rough promptings.

With an evil smile, Carl leads me to Machine Number 2.
This is an upright machine, constructed of the same chrome
and leather and equipped with a similar array of weights,
pulleys, and straps. The thought occurs to me that each of
these machines is a modern version of some medieval instrument of torture, updated and made more efficient through
computer design.

When I am fully loaded into Machine Number 2, Carl disappears again, and I find myself staring at the green concrete
block wall. Then Dr. Mangones' voice resumes over the loudspeaker.

"No, Carl was right. You did not perform well on Machine
Number One. But that is not unusual. By the time an average trainee has experienced Machine Number Twelve, he, or

she, as the case may be, has overcome his, or her, initial resistance and adjusts to the so-called pain quite satisfactorily.

"You notice how I describe the pain as so-called, and indeed it is. For our studies with prisoners of war and other incarcerants revealed that the subject's tolerance increases dramatically in proportion to the severity and the length of the treatment applied. And I'm certain you will have the same experience, because my judgment at this point is that you are a perfectly average trainee. So, you see, as your tolerance increases, the sensation of pain diminishes until it is completely gone. That is why we call it so-called pain.

"Let me interpose a thought here. We are, after all, nothing more nor less than behaviorists. We are convinced through our own experience, reinforced by a wide variety of studies, that even the most deviant behavior can be brought within normal parameters by the judicious application of carefully conceived and scrupulously executed treatment programs.

"Nor do I mean to suggest by this that your behavior has been all that deviant. But it is enough out of the mainstream of conformity to attract attention and thus produce a disruptive influence on the normal conduct of corporate business. Again, let me remind you of our benevolent purposes — not only the best interests of the corporation, but your own personal best interests as well."

Dr. Mangones switches off and the music begins again. Siegfried's journey will never end, and I am doomed to be his traveling companion on this trip through hell.

Carl, or whoever is operating the machine, starts the tape a few revolutions into the recording and has to stop, rewind, and resume again. This gives me a brief breathing spell before the next treatment session begins.

I use the time to assure myself that I can survive any torture they may invent. Machine Number 2 starts to shake violently, and I wait for some painful new phase to begin. But the shaking only increases until after a half hour or so the machine switches abruptly into a horizontal position and moves along gleaming tracks toward the wall. Then the bench I am strapped to lurches forward, and my head hits the wall with a painful bump.

"Sometimes you must feel in your work that you are beating your head against a brick wall. Well, even that can be endured." It is Dr. Mangones again, and he concludes his short commentary with a maniacal laugh. The force of the head pounding increases until the pain becomes intolerable. Before each new forward thrust, I brace myself for the blow, but it seems to do no good. Every new blow is worse than the last, and I feel the top of my head begin to swell. Then I feel blood begin to ooze from my scalp, and when the machine returns to its original position, as I prepare for the new hammer blow, I hear blood dripping to the floor beneath me.

This can't continue; they will end up killing me, I think, but I know that the treatment has only begun, that what is to follow is probably going to be worse.

Just as I expect, the pounding continues, and with every audible crack of my skull against the cement I drift further and further toward unconsciousness. The room takes on the vague aspect of a living thing that holds me in its huge, hairy arms, delivers me, almost lovingly, into the hard, rough surface of the wall, and returns me, careful not to lose its grip, to the starting position. Perhaps it is Carl himself, I think, and the machine is only an illusion. This idea is somehow comforting — the idea that I am in the hands of a living person who will eventually take pity on me, stop ramming my head into the wall, take me to a cool room, and serve me a tall, ice cold glass of beer.

The dripping of blood and sweat becomes louder and faster, like the ticking of a runaway clock. Time seems to turn in on itself so that I begin to believe with each return to the starting position that the treatment is yet to begin, that I have yet to experience the first blow. The sounds of Siegfried become fainter, and I no longer hear the noise of the dripping blood. Between the blows there is only blackness, interrupted by an explosion of light that flashes across my eyes each time the bench hurtles forward and rams my skull against the wall. This form of torture may have been used before, in the Inquisition or by the Nazis, I remember thinking between blows. But I don't remember reading about it. Right now, I don't remember anything — where I am, what exactly is happening to me, or why.

Suddenly I am aware that the machine has stopped. A voice comes over the loudspeaker:

"We are experiencing a minor malfunction in Machine Number Two. Please be patient until operation can be resumed."

The hammer blows begin anew. The familiar comfort of unconsciousness looms within reach, and I anxiously start counting each blow, hoping to drift beyond the boundary before ten more can be delivered. My hopes are answered, and I am wrapped again in blessed darkness.

When I revive this time, I am back in my suite, sprawled diagonally across the bed as if I have been thrown there by some giant. Giant, indeed — Carl. I make my way, half crawling, to the bar and pour myself a small tumbler of Scotch. I drink it neat, not having the strength to get ice from the refrigerator. Reviving slightly, I stumble to the dresser and stare at myself in the mirror. The top of my head is wrapped in a huge bandage, and the gauntness of the face I see startles me.

"Good evening, good evening," booms a voice over the speakers, the unmistakable voice of Dr. Mangones. "I hope you enjoyed your afternoon snooze — ha-ha — and that you will be ready for dinner in half an hour in the executive dining room. A technician will be arriving to escort you."

At dinner, I find myself part of a group sitting at a round table covered with white linen. We are served steak and shrimp on exquisite china by three beautiful young technicians. There is droning talk and much laughter about the play-by-play of a recent football game.

I am treated with great deference and kindness. My dinner companions, whoever they are, keep asking for my opinion, wonder whether I watched the game, and express their profound disappointment that I missed this truly outstanding event. For a brief interlude, the talk turns to resurfacing driveways and ranges widely from the costs to the relative advantages and disadvantages of certain materials and contractors.

The talk continues in a spirit of high good fellowship, interspersed with occasional kidding and a few mildly dirty stories whenever the waitresses are out of the room. My companions inquire once or twice if I am over my "headache" and keep asking whether I would like more wine. I hardly eat anything, which seems to concern them greatly. They advise me that the training will go much easier if I will only watch my diet, but they also urge me to have one of the double chocolate sundaes that the waitresses offer us.

I have great difficulty fighting back the waves of nausea that overtake me. I try to sit up straight and pretend that I am one of them, that I feel just as jolly and optimistic about everything as they do. But I know my efforts are ridiculous. By the time people start getting up from the table, I have almost fallen asleep. The next thing I know I am being helped down the corridors to my suite.

That much I remember about the dinner. But now I fall onto the bed without undressing and sink immediately into a dreamless sleep as deep as the unconsciousness I had experienced twice earlier today.

Again, a voice comes over the loudspeaker. I open my eyes to the dim nightlight.

"All reward is in the striving, all success is in surviving, all truth is in enduring," the voice booms out into the room.

Nothing follows. A short time later, or what seems to me to be a short time, the voice returns.

"The individual serves the corporation; the corporation serves the nation. Together, we serve freedom and prosperity."

So it goes through the night. As morning approaches, I no longer fall asleep between these taped messages. I watch the clock to see how often they occur. They blast out regularly at half-hour intervals — precisely, without failure, until I notice that the clock is about to reach six. Then the voice booms out again:

"Good morning. It is time to resume training. We wish you a good day. Your belief in the power of free enterprise will see you through this day. Your belief in yourself, and in the wisdom of the corporation, will inspire you to overcome whatever difficulties this day may offer. Have a successful day."

There is a knock at the door. It is a technician with breakfast. This one is more cheerful than the one who brought breakfast yesterday. Was it really only yesterday?

"Breakfast, sir." The man sets the tray on my desk and smiles a wan smile with a knowing cast, a smile that seems to recognize my suffering.

"The next session will begin in half an hour," my cheerful attendant informs me. "Please be ready for the technician who will escort you to the Trainorium."

18

I AM BACK in the Trainorium for the beginning of the second day's conditioning, sitting on the floor and waiting for the arrival of my trainer, when Dr. Mangones' voice bursts out from the speaker system. His tone this morning is not at all pleasant, not at all the neutral voice of the detached clinician that I have become used to.

"At dinner last night," he begins abruptly, "you showed a rather startling ignorance of football and certain other sports that were the accepted topics for discussion. One might excuse that on the grounds that your interests lie elsewhere. But you must learn to adopt the interests of the group in order to eliminate any possible hint of unconventionality.

"Furthermore" — Dr. Mangones' voice is becoming steadily more querulous — "you displayed no interest in nor knowledge of masculine science, that is to say, in this instance, of driveway resurfacing. As you know only too well, I am sure, this is a recurring subject of conversation in the

executive dining room, one that you are expected to familiar-
ize yourself with fully."

Then his voice softens almost imperceptibly.

"Truth to tell, I have the feeling that I should not have
brought this subject up until the Management Adaptability
Seminar. That would be a more appropriate time for us to
go into it. On the other hand, my remarks this morning will
give you a chance to think about these things. They are important, after all. Perhaps in the next few days you will be
able to show some improvement. If you will go to the trouble
of examining the books in your library, you will find a number of excellent volumes on the subjects I mentioned. I particularly call your attention to the sports statistics section of
the *World Almanac and Book of Facts* and the *Reader's Di-
gest Home Improvement Manual.*

"Let me see now. Well, I guess this is all I have to say this
morning. You will find Machines Three through Six similar
to those you experienced yesterday, although considerably
more arduous."

Dr. Mangones signs off with a sickeningly hearty "Good
luck! And have a successful day!"

He is right about Machines 3 through 6. Buoyed by the
prospect of increasing my suffering, Carl is almost cheerful
as he straps me into Machine Number 3.

"This is a new number, and we aren't quite sure yet
whether it will do the job for us," Carl informs me, tighten-
ing the buckle on my right wrist.

The day creeps into a nightmare of pain and terror, with
several lapses into unconsciousness. I lose track of the machines. It seems I am exposed to a dozen or so. One of them
jabs sharp points into my thighs and armpits. Another sends
strong electrical shocks through my body. A third whirls
me in endless circles, then plunges me into a stainless steel
tank of ice cold water, throwing me rudely back into con-

sciousness. This time nausea overcomes me, and as Carl un-
straps me from the last machine late in the afternoon, my
training uniform is covered with blood and vomit.

"You didn't do so bad today," Carl announces. "In fact, I
would say you're pretty much up to normal trainee performance."

Again, Carl pushes me back to my suite, where I crumble,
exhausted and sobbing, onto the bed. Perhaps because of my
vomiting I am hungry, and I find myself actually looking
forward to dinner with the sports and home maintenance en-
thusiasts. I want to sleep, but I toss wildly on the bed, aching
in every bone. Finally, I pull myself up from the bed and
make my way to the bookshelf, where I find the *World Almanac and Book of Facts* Dr. Mangones recommended.

I fall into the easy chair and begin thumbing through the
sports section. My eyelids are heavy as I browse through the
pages of names and figures, but I concentrate on memorizing
random facts. I have enough sense to avoid offbeat sports such
as curling, lacrosse, or water polo, sticking to mainstream subjects such as football and baseball. I have always been good
at memorizing such useless facts quickly, and after an hour
I am silently reciting a whole battery of amazing sports
achievements to myself in preparation for the approaching
dinner.

When I take my place at the table, I find I am in much
better shape than I was the night before. Perhaps the theory
of the training staff is sound: the first day is the hardest, and
the trainee becomes more and more able to tolerate the increasingly difficult stages of torture.

In any event, I find myself conscious enough to look carefully at the faces of my companions. And so I notice, for the
first time, that they look amazingly alike — all square-jawed,
all tall, large-boned, and athletic. As a group, they remind me
of the people I saw on a visit years ago to Salt Lake City —

rugged, pioneer-type Mormons with an astoundingly homogeneous look about them.

I realize, of course, that this likeness is heightened by the identical blue suits my companions are wearing. But still, there is not a short man among them, not a black, and not one pair of glasses to be seen.

While I tear my way into the shrimp cocktail and swallow great gulps of the Chablis, I speculate whether any of them are also trainees. If any of them are, they are very good at concealing their agony behind their pleasant half smiles.

"Of course, you have to realize that with the Japanese, you're dealing with an entirely different culture. We taught them many of the same management practices that we are now admiring, taught them all this back in the forties. So this is nothing new. You can't expect our production workers to sing songs in the morning. Most of them are hung over and thinking about going deer hunting or fishing," one of the heartiest of the group is saying.

"Yes, but I still think there's a lot of good stuff in *Theory Z*. Did you read it?" another asks.

The conversation rolls on. I wait for my chance. It arrives soon in the form of a brief silence.

"Say, does anyone know if anybody's topped Jim Bakken's field goal record — in one game — the Cardinals versus the Steelers in sixty-seven I think it was," I inquire, trying to make it sound like the kind of question I ask frequently.

My colleagues look around at each other but do not appear surprised.

"Gee, no. I think that still stands. Do you know, Walt?"

"As far as I know. Yeah, I think so. You follow football pretty closely?"

"Well, I guess so," I reply, trying to look modest. "I'm not the expert some of you guys are, but I do watch a lot of games."

"Well, welcome to the club."

There is a round of raucous laughter. I feel better about myself, begin to feel as if these people may be on my side. Maybe the corporation is right; maybe I should have tried all along to put myself into the mainstream.

The conversation continues — most of it about sports. I feel good, because I have given them the text for the day. For the first time since I started my training, I begin to believe in the possibility of being accepted. This makes me more optimistic that I can endure what the next few days may hold for me.

19

WHAT THE NEXT FEW DAYS hold for me is more of the same, five more days of "workout" on the machines. The machines are marvels of technology. A rack that is computerized, its pull diminishing or increasing to correspond to changes in the subject's vital signs. An electric chair that provides its occupant with a video display of the fluctuating current. A steel couch that is refrigerated, retaining pieces of the subject's skin as he is unstrapped. Stereo earphones that increase the sound level to just before the point of irreparable ear damage before switching to a tolerable level. A tank into which steam is pumped at scalding temperatures. An oxygen tank in which the level of oxygen is barely enough to sustain life but where the little remaining air is scented with changing fragrances. And finally, worst of all, a "sperm gauge" in which a rubber finger massages the prostate until a "sample" is produced, whereupon a large video display provides the subject with a digital readout of his sperm count.

"The Company is looking for a few good men," Carl says

with a chuckle as he removes me from this final instrument of torture. "Doesn't look like you'll make it. You're way too low."

The long nightmare of Positive Attitudinal Reinforcement is over. I am through, apparently, with the days of thin soup as I sit, drifting back into consciousness, in the grim private dining room where I am given lunch. I am through with the endless slogans that spill out of the Trainorium's speaker system. I am through, once and for all, with the vapid conversations and the dull laughter of my dinner companions. And, with any luck at all, I can count myself through with sleepless nights interrupted by the witless pronouncements of Dr. Mangones from the television set.

When I am summoned to appear before the committee that will review my progress, I catch a glimpse of myself in the mirror — a shocking glimpse of a man transformed, the survivor of some new and undiscovered Buchenwald. Pale, gaunt, almost lifeless, but clean-shaven and dressed in a fresh, crisp blue uniform, I am pushed, pulled, half carried into the conference room with its huge oak table, water carafes, and blank faces that stare at me with no sign of sympathy or recognition.

There are five reviewers, inquisitors, judges — whatever one wants to call them. I can tell nothing from their faces or from other aspects of their appearance. They all look the same, and all are wearing exactly the same kind of uniform that I have on.

Are these men all Ph.D. psychologists, all classmates, perhaps, from Columbia? But wait, is it possible that these are the same men I have eaten dinner with for the last five nights? It's really impossible to tell anything about them, at least until they speak. And even after I have heard their voices, I realize they all sound alike, use the same vocabulary, the Business BASIC that is becoming so familiar to me.

Dr. Mangones enters the room and takes a seat facing me at the other end of the table. He is ominously cheerful.

"Well," he says, pulling a stack of papers from his briefcase and spreading them over the table, "what have we here? Yes. Hmmmm. Not so good. Yes. Some improvement. A disaster. Yes.

"Well, altogether, I can sum up by saying that you are not the least successful trainee we have had in our midst. But certainly you are not the most successful. By the way, is English your native language?"

"Why, yes, Dr. Mangones, of course," I mutter.

"The reason I ask is that there are certain unnatural elisions, certain guttural lapses, and a persistent difficulty with your *s*'s that must be overcome. Then, too, the voice level itself is far above the level of executive pitch. Far too high. Your sentences have an inordinately high hesitation count, and there are other substandard qualities. You will need a lot of work there."

"Yes, of course."

"And posture. We must give you extra time in our Posturium. You will like it there — the technicians are women. Ha-ha.

"Well, we do not drag out these evaluations. Overall, I believe your response to attitudinal training has been satisfactory. On the positive side, the observers report a heightened interest in approved conversational topics, and one respondent — I guess there are two — reports the occasional appearance of a standard near-smile." Dr. Mangones looks up. "You understand what a near-smile is?"

"Yes, yes I think I do. I've been working on it." I try to produce one on the spot, but I know that it is a failure.

"You observers — do any of you disagree with a 'satisfactory' performance rating at this point? No? Good. Well then, I think we are ready to proceed with the next phase of training."

Dr. Mangones glides into a long explanation of Extra-corporate Environment Norms (EEN). His presentation is full of highly stylized gibberish lifted verbatim from some management guide, and I find myself having to fight back sleep. He explains that the employee's behavior is just as important to the corporation outside the workplace as when he is working. He confides that the Company has no intention of limiting the employee's freedom while off duty, but that certain standards are important if the Company's reputation is to be maintained.

When he finishes, there is silence, and the room suddenly grows dark. A screen is lowered into place on the wall behind his head, and he moves aside. It is a large screen, and suddenly it is filled with the picture of a naked man rolling on the floor of an office, wrestling with three naked women.

There is sound. The man is drunk. He is barking like a dog. The women are laughing. The man picks up a bottle of champagne, shakes it vigorously, and squirts it at one of the women. He takes a couple of swallows, then suddenly slumps over and falls asleep.

I know from the instant the picture appears on the screen and the sound begins that I am the man in the film. When the lights come on and the screen disappears, there is an embarrassed clearing of throats. Dr. Mangones moves back to his place at the head of the table.

"The film speaks for itself," he says, lowering his voice almost imperceptibly. "Obviously, in your case EEN will be one of the most important parts of this training. We will be watching you with special vigilance during this phase, and I am hopeful that your performance will be better than it was in the first phase. The review is over."

That night I have the first decent sleep since training began. I can't account for the fact of no interruptions, but I know the night's deep sleep comes just on the verge of my total collapse. Perhaps it was planned this way.

20

WHEN I WALK into the EEN training room, I am stunned to see Barbara Burdoch sprawled over a white silk couch, almost unrecognizable. Gone is the plain dark skirt, the demure blouse, the no-nonsense jacket. What we have here is Barbara the seductress in her own special uniform — a tight, pale blue silk jumpsuit with the corporate logo at the epicenter of her left breast. From the moment I enter her training quarters, I understand Barbara's assignment — to assure that I will never again repeat my indiscretions in Los Angeles.

Incredibly, Barbara pretends that we have never met, never sat together in endless meetings with Marlott and Stelritz. And incredibly, for reasons I cannot explain, I go along with her game.

It's almost impossible to avoid saying something about our previous life together, but I resist the temptation. For one thing, I doubt if Barbara would admit to it. For another, I am too interested in seeing how this other Barbara will behave.

Barbara's teaching style proves to be in sharp contrast to Dr. Mangones'. He is every bit the company psychologist, cool and detached. She is the quintessential mistress, warm, grateful, accommodating, eager to please.

"Come on, let's have something to drink," she says after we get through the preliminary chatter about what this phase of the training will entail.

"No, I don't think so, not this time."

"Not this time? Was there another time?"

"No, of course not. I just mean I don't feel like it now."

"But come on. I know how tough the course has been so far. Our policy is to encourage people to relax."

"No, really. I'm not in the mood right now."

"What mood are you in, then?"

"Just the mood to finish this as quickly as possible and get back to my job upstairs."

"Surely you don't find this unpleasant? Come over here and sit beside me."

"Actually, I'm pretty comfortable here."

"Then I'll come over to you." She sits on the arm of my chair, her arms around my neck.

"Look, if you think I'm going to get involved in sex play, you're crazy. I know that all of this is being taped, and I know that it's a violation of company rules to engage in sex on company property — or with anyone other than one's spouse anywhere, for that matter."

"That's ridiculous. Who told you that? There is no way the Company could enforce such an outrageous policy." Barbara's look of astonishment appears genuine.

"Well, I happen to know that it's true. I read all the directives and follow these things closely."

Barbara ignores me. She begins stroking me gently, caressing my face and kissing it. Then she unzips my uniform down to my waist and reaches inside. I feel her hand, cold and businesslike, doing the business of seduction. But I can only think of the machines, think about the punishment I will get if I fail to resist her. Barbara appears excited, but her behavior has an artificial quality to it. I know that she has learned how to appear aroused, just as a prostitute would, and I know that everything she is doing now — every gentle touch, every apparently spontaneous movement — is only part of a carefully devised program designed to shatter even the strongest resistance.

"Actually," Barbara murmurs, "the Company wants you to have fun, wants you to relax. Can't you relax for just a few minutes? I can assure you that we're completely alone here. Let me remind you that this phase of our training is designated Extra-corporate Environment Norms. Now, what does 'norms' mean to you? Why, it means, of course, how most of the Company's employees would behave in a situation like this. So let yourself go. Doesn't this feel good? Here, let's zip that down a little more. I think you'd be more comfortable."

Barbara tries everything imaginable — and some things that had been unimaginable. Her style shifts — too abruptly, I'm afraid — from the girl in the back seat of the car to the convention call girl to the woman you meet in the airport bar who has just enough time between planes. She tries silence, then conversation, ranging from the most outrageous obscenities to sublime quotations from ancient love poetry. She changes her pace, varies her breathing, blows her warm breath on different parts of my body, strokes, massages, whispers, cajoles, laughs, pleads, and finally cries, her body bathed in sweat. I remain an impenetrable fortress through the simple device of concentrating on Machines 3 and 7, the worst in my memory. In the midst of her seduction, I feel only the pain of the icy water, the electricity surging through my testicles. I am proving exactly what the Company would like me to prove, that given the right attitude, I can resist even the most skillful seductress that money can buy.

Exhausted, Barbara collapses on the floor, breathing heavily, moaning in frustration. For the first time I realize that she is genuinely aroused, and I feel a faint sense of pity for her.

"You sonofabitch," she moans, her voice low and raspy. "You miserable faggot. You fucking eunuch. You realize this has never happened before? You filthy bastard. You realize this is all on tape? Are you aware this could cost me my job?"

"I'm sorry, Barbara," I say, stroking her hair. "I'm really very sorry, but it is, as you know, against company policy to be caught engaging in extracurricular sex. And that, as you know, is because the Company encourages a normal family life and the maintenance of the marital relationship. Happy, satisfied wives are essential to the efficient performance of their husbands. Oh, I should have said spouses — that was a little sexist. Happy, satisfied spouses are essential to the efficient performance of their spouses, or something like that."

Barbara gets up slowly, straightens out her uniform, sits down on a couch opposite me, and reaches for a legal pad on the table beside her. She scribbles furiously for at least five minutes, then puts the pad back on the table.

She faces me with a look of pure hatred.

"Now get the hell out of here," she breathes, her voice hardly audible. "Your EEN training is completed. You have passed. Normally, this part of the training takes three days. Nobody in the history of the Troubled Employee Department has ever completed it in less than two days. And even though you have passed, by the standards I'm supposed to follow, I am recommending that you be discharged from the Company immediately. Do you hear me? Discharged."

It is the first time I am allowed to return to my quarters unescorted, Barbara's being in too much of a hurry to wait for an escort. It is also the first time I recall laughing, or even smiling, since my arrival in the department just a week earlier. When I am back in my suite, I pour myself a stiff drink and sit laughing uncontrollably, thinking of the committee as it watches the tape of Barbara and me.

21

SUPERVISORY APTITUDE DEVELOPMENT proves to be wonderfully easy compared with what has gone before. For one thing, this part of the program is shaped to fit individual needs. In my case, Dr. Mangones explains, I am to be given special attention in such basics as Posture Control, Executive Stride, and Executive Smile, which I have long recognized as one of my greatest weaknesses.

At this point in the program, the training also shifts abruptly from the "correction" to the "recognition" mode, Dr. Mangones explains. This means that my trainers now use the carrot rather than the stick.

Another advantage here is that one has several different classes every day, instead of concentrating on only one "subject." This provides the academic variety, if not the physical variety, of the college campus. And at this point there is another important step toward normalcy. I am given a navy blue blazer and gray slacks to wear to the sessions. Even though the blazer displays the company logo above the pocket, it is a great improvement over the dark blue uniform I had been wearing.

One learns quickly not to confuse "posture" with "posturing." The most difficult thing about my posture class is that the emphasis is on assuming the body position most appropriate for the circumstances without appearing conscious of the effort involved.

The Posturium is a simple room, about the size of a conference room, and done up in a basic businesslike style, without frills. The idea here is to re-create exactly the environment of a working meeting, I am told. The designers have gone so far as to create very lifelike dummies who sit in the appropriate attitude, most of them looking attentively at the head of the table, where the speaker sits. One ingenious aspect of this tableau is that there are several sets of dummies. One set consists largely of peers, another of subordinates (a difficult audience to gather, in my case), and a third entirely of superiors. Again, the realism of these dummies is astounding. For instance, the subordinate dummies sit in a very attentive position, their faces turned toward the speaker, their hands posed as if to record every vital word. The peer dummies are somewhat slouched, not altogether inattentive, but enough so to show their boredom and mild disapproval. They do not take notes. The superior dummies are fully slouched and relaxed, but their faces are turned toward me (the speaker) and drawn to resemble full and critical attention. A few of the superior dummies appear to be taking notes. As I understand the situation, the idea is that these dummy note-takers have been asked to evaluate what I have to say and report to their superiors.

The effect of this training is uncannily realistic. One learns right away that one must adapt his (or her) posture and demeanor to fit the situation. One quickly learns that the proper posture to adopt is very close to a reverse image of the group posture. For example, when one is facing a table of superior dummies, or dummy superiors, one must assume a very straight, alert, smart, and respectful posture. When one is confronted by a group of subordinates, one must slump appropriately into one's chair and avoid looking directly at any of the audience. Finally, in company with one's peers, one is supposed to eye each of them face to face, one's position somewhat between a casual slouch and a more respectful vertical.

This description gives only the broadest view of what is, indeed, a refined and sophisticated discipline. Each of the situations is altered, in practice, with a wide variety of differing circumstances. Obviously, one must learn the proper demeanor for a mixed audience of peers and subordinates. Then, too, the requirements vary for different texts. A bad report demands a more aggressive stance; a good one, naturally, a more subdued, even humble, attitude. "Posture" is not a very accurate designation for this part of the training, because the course includes facial expression, hand position, eye contact, movement tempo, and other aspects of body language. It is a fascinating course, and it doesn't take me long to get enthusiastic about it. Much of the committee's critique consists of viewing videotapes of one's performance, and I am pleased. So, too, apparently, are Dr. Mangones and the committee. In fact, at one point the entire committee, led by Dr. Mangones, breaks into applause.

"A most original, subtle, and effective arrangement," Dr. Mangones says, ordering the projectionist to stop the tape. "Notice the hands folded in a prayerlike position, the almost imperceptible tilt of the head, which denotes total attention without being blatantly offensive. Here is talent, gentlemen, talent and promise. We are pleased."

The group again breaks into applause, and I am ecstatic.

Gone, momentarily at least, is the agonizing memory of my days in Positive Attitudinal Reinforcement, the sharp, hot, painful, unconscious hours on the machines. Gone too are the negative feelings I had for Barbara Burdoch. In this moment of triumph, I see a fleeting image of her voluptuous body, and my revulsion changes to lust. My whole body surges with a feeling of executive strength. My eyes begin to fill with tears as I hear the group break into another round of applause when Dr. Mangones, his voice the proud teacher's, comments enthusiastically on the bored, distracted look I gave a group of subordinates.

Much to my surprise, I find myself almost as positive about Executive Voice as I was about Posture. But not quite, because you don't have the fun of seeing your performance. Also, the endless listening for inflection, interrupted repeatedly by the instructor's commentary, can become quite boring.

My main problem, I learn, sitting in the soundproofed Audiotorium, is one of pitch. I am given tapes of anonymous leading executives from many different branches of business — finance, transportation, service, food, heavy industry, and so forth. There are subtle variations among these types, but there is also an impressive uniformity, the deep, resounding, slow resonance of the "confident voice" (the norm one must achieve in order to pass this section of the training).

My instructor keeps at me to develop what he refers to as the "orotund quality." And I keep asking him what he means by this. His explanations are vague and useless. Finally, after repeated questions on my part, he reads a passage from an old book that apparently was a favorite of the Founder's:

> Orotund is a mode of intonation directly from the larynx, which gives fullness, clearness, and strength. The highest perfection of voice, it is used in solemn, pathetic, energetic,

and vehement forms of expression. The Orotund usually admits of three degrees, designated according to the intensity of the emotion: Effusive, or the language of solemnity and pathos; Expulsive, or the language of earnest declamation; Explosive, or the language of intense passion.

But the orotund quality, my instructor explains, is to be used only sparingly, when I am urging a course of action on my superiors or, more commonly, when I am trying to inspire subordinates. A more useful mode is something called "pure tone." Again, my instructor refers me to the Founder's old book:

> Pure Tone is free from any harsh, guttural, aspirated, nasal, or oral tone, and is made with less expenditure of breath, and with less fatigue, than any other.
> The essentials to purity of Tone are deep breathing, control of the muscles of the throat regulating the vocal organs, and a free opening of the mouth.
> A great cause of impurity of Tone is the expulsion of too much breath. To test its purity, in this respect, hold the back of the hand within an inch or two of the mouth while uttering the sound, and if a current of air from the mouth is perceptible by the hand, the tone is not pure.
> Pure Tone is used in unimpassioned discourse; in the expression of light and agreeable emotions; and in sadness or grief when not mingled with solemnity.

I have an especially difficult time mastering the principal forms of Stance, which as far as I can understand is really nothing more than an older way of describing body language. There are several forms I have to master, including Admiraton, Appeal, Caution, Disdain, Modesty, and Resolution. The instructions for all of these modes differ, of course, but here is an example for Modesty, again taken from the Founder's old book:

The right foot set fairly on the ground; the left heel a little lifted; the right arm at full length, but a few inches from the side; the hand open, the back of the hand in front; the left arm close to the body to the elbow; the forearm a little extended from the body, but tending downward; the hand open; the palm downward. This attitude and gesture will express modesty and respect for the persons addressed.

My instructor seems to consider this mode as one of the most useful in the program, so we work very hard at getting it just right. I spend endless hours frozen in this position, with the instructor sitting in an easy chair a few feet away, making subtle corrections over and over again.

"Lower that left heel just a hair," he says. "There, that's good. Now, no, your right arm is not quite right, a little more to the left. Perfect. Just right. Very, very modest indeed."

I have special trouble with what is described (in the strange dialect of the department) as Humblepause. This is a lifelong habit that must be erased in the few remaining days, and it is most difficult. Also, closely connected with this impediment, is my penchant for Gropesounds, the *er*'s and *ah*'s so common to many speakers searching for the right word. My instructor explains repeatedly and with great patience that the so-called correct words are not nearly so important as the appearance of confidence and conviction.

"Look, what you are saying is not going to be written down, and in most cases it will have little effect on the course of company business," he says. "What is important to the Executive Aspirant is what one might call Executive Mystique — the projection of confidence and control."

So I labor away, with surprising success, at lowering my voice to the deepest register and eliminating all signs that might point to doubt or hesitation, or even to the trivial and irrelevant compulsion to find the "right" word. One is given certain Helpprops, such things as a pipe and a pointer to use with charts. I have never smoked a pipe in my life, and I find it somewhat hard to get used to. Of course, the pipe is not lit because of certain fire regulations applying to the department. But I find after much awkward fumbling and dropping that the pipe becomes something of a scepter — it gives me a feeling of office and the power that goes with it. I am amused that Dr. Mangones compliments me when I pretend to light the pipe. He points out that the time I took for this process was exactly right for the peer and subordinate groups. (He was especially complimentary of the way I cleaned it during a peer group meeting. Of course, one is forbidden to use the pipe when one is meeting with a group of superiors.)

Executive Smile is not nearly as difficult as I had expected. This whole problem has been reduced to a matter of angles and form, a bioengineering matter, really. It does take a certain amount of practice to maintain this unnatural expression for any length of time. But you can develop the ability through practice and by certain easy exercises.

The most difficult thing for me is Executive Stride. Conrad and I had talked jokingly about developing the perfect Executive Shuffle, to be used when approaching Marlott's desk or leaving his office.

I was surprised, then, to discover that our fantasy was not so far from reality. Because, as I found out two days into this class, Executive Stride has certain variations, and one of them is, indeed, the proper way to enter and leave a superior's office.

Once more I am taught that subtlety is everything. Time and again, I overcompensate to the point that my movements are almost a caricature of the ideal. Just as an example, the Executive Shuffle that Conrad and I proposed is really more of a subdued Corridor Stride, not nearly so purposeful and fast, but lacking none of the businesslike quality that marks the way successful executives move from office to office. The Executive Shuffle cannot be obvious! The proper exit consists of an exactly timed period of standing before the Turn and Walkout are executed. It is during this Respectstand that one listens to additional details of the superior's instructions and gives assurances that everything will be done exactly as ordered. Then, and only then, does the careful about-face occur. The exit should not be that of a servant overcome by awe and humility, but that of the loyal functionary hurrying to carry out his mission.

As the week wears on, I continue to receive high praise for my progress in Executive Voice and Executive Posture, but my progress in Executive Stride is slow and disappointing. I am given special instruction by a burly technician in the gym, which has its own track, with carpets and walls matching those of the corridors on the floors above us. This husky instructor, who I was told had once been a member of some Olympic track team, follows close behind me, occasionally giving me a shove after checking his stopwatch or stopping me to straighten my shoulders. He is brusque and unpleasant, and the more we work together, the less progress I seem to make.

"Confidence, purpose, determination," he shouts as I march along, and the more he shouts, the less confidence, purpose, and determination I seem to feel. Once, in a fit of rage, he gives me a painful kick, then apologizes sullenly.

"If you would only do what I tell you to do instead of loping along like a professor. This isn't a college campus, for Christ's sake! This is one of the ten largest corporations in the world! Walk with pride, walk with purpose, walk as if every step increased our profits!" he screams.

I try to think of it as a walk for charity. It is as if every turn around the track with my demanding trainer means ten more dollars for crippled children or some other group of unfortunates. Only in this case I am the unfortunate. One more lap around the track, accompanied by the kicks, shoves, and screams of my "coach," means money for me. Thousands of dollars, perhaps, if I am able to complete this phase of the training successfully, "graduate" to my old job upstairs, and start the move upward that could, very possibly, lead even to a vice presidency.

But the going is tough. At the first committee meeting, there is an embarrassed silence after the videotapes of my final exam are shown.

Trying to be as diplomatic as possible, Dr. Mangones clears his voice and speaks in a soft, sympathetic drawl, his near-whisper of support and confidentiality:

"Is it possible, without your knowing it, that you had polio as a small child? Or were you perhaps teased mercilessly by older boys on the way to school?"

I feel the onset of rage, but I control my voice. "No, Dr. Mangones, none of that."

"I see. Well, let's be honest. Your walk resembles most closely that of a Chilean peasant, high in the Andes, struggling home with a load of firewood on his back. Do you see what I mean? Take another look at this tape. Let's have it again."

The tape is run a second time. I try to look at my walk critically, but I see nothing uncommon about it. But then, I am used to my own walk. I have observed myself in countless plate glass windows over the years; I have seen myself in home movies.

"You see what I mean?" Dr. Mangones demands when the tape is over.

"Yes, sir. I think I do."

"Then work on it. Get with it. You need at least three more days. This means the customary two-week period of your training will have to be extended. But there is no other way. We do not fail people here. Nobody fails. We work with them until they succeed. Is that clear?"

Dr. Mangones' ultimatum is a blow worse than any I have received at the hands of a machine. Three more days of Rupert the walking coach.

The three days go slowly, a blur of bruising kicks and shouted obscenities. But as the time moves ponderously by, I notice a gradual improvement in Rupert's spirits.

"Good. Good," Rupert shouts. "You have it. You have the Executive Stride! I knew you had it in you. Now, let's run through that again. This time use the briefcase. It gives you additional balance and poise."

When the committee meets to review the new set of tapes, it is ecstatic.

"A miracle, Rupert, a miracle," Dr. Mangones purrs. "You have done the impossible. This man has the walk of a vice president — even a president. You took a hopeless case and transformed it into a champion. Congratulations, Rupert!"

Again, the committee breaks into applause. They are looking at Rupert and smiling; apparently none of the credit is to be given to me. I am indifferent; the important thing is to be done with Rupert, finished with the whole Supervisory Aptitude Development phase, and ready to begin the fourth and final phase of my extended training in the department, the Management Adaptability Seminar.

22

I HAVE THREE IMPORTANT DREAMS during this last phase of the training, dreams that expand the twilight between reality and illusion.

In the first, I am invited to the Chairman's living quarters for cocktails and dinner, a reward for outstanding work. The details of this dream are obscure, but I do recall the Chairman's smiling face, the attention of the servants, and, above all, the Chairman's German shepherd lying beside a deep blue couch in the huge living room. Not any German shepherd, in my memory of this dream, but the same German shepherd that sat at my desk and disappeared just before I had a chance to prove his existence to Conrad. Nor is it only the markings that convince me it is the same dog; the Chairman's German shepherd greets me like an old friend, wagging his tail and licking my hand. And that is not the only way this dream reaches back to reality.

Immediately after dinner, the Chairman grabs me by the

arm, leads me to his private elevator, and takes me up onto the building's roof. There, under a moon that gives the Chairman's face a ghostly pallor, he proudly shows me his prize pigeons, cooing and fluttering around coops that must be the most luxurious in the world. The pigeons I also recognize as old friends — the same pigeons, I am sure, that burst out from behind the guards' station and nearly frightened me to death. The guards had denied their existence, but here they are in the Chairman's keeping in a dream so clear that it is real.

The second dream is about the suppliers speech, the Formula for the Future speech in which the chief chemist disappears behind a screen, supposedly to drink from a vial filled with various chemicals representing the Company's golden future. According to the script, the chemist is supposed to emerge from behind the screen wearing the hideous Founder's mask that I bought on my insane shopping expedition with Scarafini. But the dream does not follow the script at all. The Chairman gives his speech, a speech that is little more than gibberish, and the chief chemist pours various chemicals into the vial at the appropriate places in the script. Smiling a mischievous smile, the Chairman motions the chief chemist behind the screen and announces that he will drink from the vial.

But the chief chemist does not reappear immediately. In fact, several minutes pass before an aide pokes his head around the side of the screen to see why he is taking so long. The aide lets out a highly audible gasp, and several other assistants rush to see what has happened. Joining the crowd, I look down to see the chief chemist's crumpled body sprawled on the floor, several of the assistants working frantically to revive him. A team from our Medical Department rushes into the luncheon room with equipment and a stretcher. Gently, they put the chief chemist on the stretcher and hurry out the door. The Chairman, still smiling, makes some vague comment in an attempt to gloss over the incident, something like, "Well, I guess we'd better rehearse that one again." As the dream ends, I am standing outside the front door of a funeral home, watching a group from the Chemical Department carry the chief chemist's casket toward the waiting hearse.

The third dream is the most disturbing of all. It has a special quality of brightness and clarity, a greater sense of time and place than reality itself. In this dream I am back in Los Angeles, drinking in the Club Majorca with Ron. There is a blank space, and when the dream resumes, I am sitting in a lavish hall of Oriental splendor, its floors covered with exquisite Persian rugs and its walls with expensive paintings. Behind an enormous teak desk sits a man so shriveled with age that it seems the mere opening of a door would blow him off his chair. This shrunken ancient is talking in a hardly audible voice while music from the third act of *Tannhäuser* fills the room. The old man's voice has the patience of a prophet's, and it drones on interminably while I stand a few feet in front of him. Strangely, even now I can recall most of what he said.

"The corporation is the highest achievement of man," the old man is saying, "the last stage of man's development. We went from man the hunter to man the warrior to man the peasant to man the tradesman to man the industrial slave. But only in the recently developed corporation have we discovered how to utilize man's energies and talents to the greatest extent possible. The genius of the corporation is its unique ability to preserve the vital talents of the individual, to harness those talents in a collective structure where the force of many can be directed toward one goal. *E pluribus unum,* so to speak.

"Of course, the corporation is not for everyone. We recognize that and accept it fully. There is a natural law at work here, because we find that those who reject the corporation are precisely those whom the corporation would want to reject. The pain comes when the inevitable rejection is only brewing, so to speak, before the incompatibility has been disclosed. Usually, that does not take long, but there are certain individuals who pose problems for us. These are individuals like yourself whose abilities are sufficiently great to justify retraining — special efforts to erase once and for all those vestiges of the infantile ego that cannot accept post-individual methods and goals."

At one point, while the old man pauses for breath, I think the end has come. Whether the music has become louder or his voice weaker, I have to step closer to the desk and lean low to hear his final words.

The old man looks at me with tears in his eyes and speaks in a whisper choked with phlegm:

"You may be the last of the candidates, the last one they send that I am able to receive. You should remember this moment as the critical turning point of your entire life, remember it because I am passing on to you a kind of grail, an invisible symbol to carry while you and others work to strengthen our corporation, work to make it a model for the entire world.

"You know, of course, that it is a kind of last crusade, what you are involved in. For the communists have taken the corporate idea and transformed it into an abomination. They have distorted entirely the idea of the corporation by eliminating the individual altogether. Tragically, this abominable creature they have invented threatens to overwhelm the world. Only America can preserve the corporation as a living entity. Only America can spread the bounty of the corporation to the less fortunate nations of the world."

The old man is through, and his head slumps against the

desk. But his eyes are still open, and he looks up at me with a look of despair and hope. I lean closer and turn my head so that my right ear is only an inch or two from his mouth. I can feel his cold breath, smell the odor of death.

"Take the torch," he gasps. "Do not disappoint me, do not fail me, for I am your Founder."

When I awoke from the dream, I knew the Founder was in the room with me, in my own bedroom behind the closed and locked door of Room 111. I could not shake the dream for days, and even now it keeps coming back to me. I work desperately to fill the gap between the Club Majorca and the Founder's mansion, but it remains intact. The gap seems to be the only barrier between the dream as fantasy and the dream as reality. If only I could fill in the gap, remember how Ron or whoever he was managed to get me from the Club Majorca to the Founder's home, then I would never again doubt that I had actually met the Founder during that strange trip to Los Angeles, not just dreamed I had. And, confirming this meeting, I would no longer have to wonder about the purpose of my mysterious journey.

23

THE FINAL PHASE of my training begins ominously. First there is a particularly intimidating pep talk from Dr. Mangones, who stresses the special difficulties of this last segment of the program. He compares it to the assault on the summit of Everest, the oral exams for a doctorate in philosophy at Harvard, and so forth.

"But you know, I have every faith in you," he says. "With the exception of the slow start and the troubles you had with the Executive Stride, I would say your progress has been more than satisfactory. So get to it and finish the course in a way that will bring credit to yourself, and the department as well."

Dr. Mangones' speech is mildly reassuring, but I am worried about the physical I am given just before MAS is to begin.

"Just a little check-up to see how you're doing," the unctuous doctor says, probing for a vein from which to draw blood. "This is perfectly routine, perfectly routine. Have you been having normal bowel movements?"

Apparently I pass the physical, because I am sent back to my room and told to get a good night's sleep for the start of MAS first thing in the morning.

Despite my apprehension about the final phase, I am relaxed, cheerful, and aggressive that night at dinner. Using my new Executive Voice, I launch into a long and rather detailed account of various engine-tuning techniques that seems to hold my companions in thrall.

"New spark plugs alone can increase fuel economy by three percent," I tell them. "When I talk about heat range, I'm talking about the capacity of the plug to conduct heat away from the firing end. The conduction must be even, in order to prevent pre-ignition. But at the same time the temperature must be high enough to burn off deposits that might create an irregular firing situation.

"Incidentally, despite what you may have heard, you don't have to change the air filter every time you tune the engine. That's a bunch of garbage. All you have to do is stick a light behind it. If you can see through the filter, you can keep on using it."

My dinner colleagues appear pleased with this information, making various comments and contributing anecdotes from their own experiences with tune-ups. They eat their sirloin steaks with abandon, order seconds, and ask for a special wine to celebrate the last phase of my training.

"We hear your progress is excellent and that you are earning especially high marks for Executive Sociability," says the man who appears to be the leader of the group, a tall, athletic blond in his fifties.

"Sociability? I don't remember that part of the training," I respond.

"Well, you've been getting it — right here. We are the sociability training group. I bet you didn't know that, did you?"

Everybody laughs.

"No, I certainly didn't, but if I'd known that, I don't think I would have said anything." Everybody starts laughing again.

"Well, don't worry about it. Actually, you've done just fine. I don't think I'm breaking confidentiality by informing you right now that the group has agreed to give you an A in Conversational Appropriateness, an A– in Executive Humor, and an A in Sports Expertise."

The group applauds. Perhaps they have had too much wine, but I am touched. In fact, I find myself warming to these men, thinking that my first reaction to them as a collection of Babbitts had been a bit harsh.

"Anyway," continues the leader, "we want to wish you the best of luck tomorrow. Don't let things get to you. What you encounter as you enter this final phase will be a bit of a shock, but we know you will do just fine."

"Well," I say, "let me use this occasion to thank each of you for your warmth and sympathy. I came in here as a novice, and I think each of you guys went out of your way to make me feel a part of the group. The training has been difficult, but your support — knowing you guys are behind me all the way — has made the whole course a lot easier."

24

MY INSTRUCTOR for the final segment of my training is a very young man with horn-rimmed glasses and eyes that seem to cut through me. He is, obviously, wholly dedicated to the Company, the kind of young fanatic who knows he will get to the top and crackles with impatience at the time it will take.

"The purpose of the Management Adaptability Seminar, or MAS," my young instructor explains, "is to prepare the executive trainee for the pressures of an increasingly competitive marketplace.

"As you certainly realize, our Company held a dominant position in the industry for many years, a position so strong that we drifted into — how shall I put it? — a slough of complacency.

"The Japanese invasion of the American marketplace changed all that. From the ashes of World War Two, Japan emerged as the industrial Gargantua of the eighties, a serious threat to smokestack America.

"We recognize, of course, that the Japanese worker represents a culture of discipline, loyalty, obedience, and stoicism that is the product of many, many centuries, and that there could be no hope of duplicating that culture in this country without a major political revolution. That revolution may, indeed, occur, but it may be a long time in coming.

"In the meantime, we took the position here at the Company that while we could not replicate the Japanese culture on a national level, we could duplicate certain important aspects of it within the limited confines of our own organization.

"For that reason, our training here in the department is aimed at instilling the very qualities of the Japanese employee that have made him such a superb instrument of capitalism. And of course, as you know, I am not talking about production line workers only. I am talking about executives. Because the conviction is that once our executives begin displaying the same qualities that have been so instrumental in the Japanese industrial resurgence, our production line workers will behave in the same fashion.

"You see, it's all a matter of productivity, which is the bottom line of industrial society. And, as you surely know, the growth in productivity in U.S. industry has lagged far behind the productivity growth of our trading rivals.

"All of this may have been explained to you at the beginning of the training, but I feel it is appropriate to repeat it this morning as you are about to begin the most rigorous phase of the course."

"Excuse me," I interrupt. "You say this is the most rigorous part? What about the machines?"

"The machines were aimed simply at raising the level of tolerance for suffering. The designers of the program believed that to be a necessary prerequisite for this rather rigorous training, which will equip you to inflict suffering and anguish on subordinates without suffering yourself.

"Now, that may not be clear to you at this point, but it will become very clear in a few minutes, when the sessions begin. I'm not suggesting that the focus of this phase will be on psychological endurance alone. You will see as you move further into this segment that we have developed an unusual combination of techniques to develop both physical and psychological strength."

Everything this young fascist says makes me more nervous about the final phase of the training. After last night's dinner, which ended in a round of drunken toasts and singing, I had been feeling very confident about my ability to endure anything they would throw at me. But today, facing this severe young man and trying to ignore a stubborn headache, I am beginning to doubt my ability to pass this final test.

"In any event," the young man continues, "I have every confidence in your capacity to survive this most rigorous phase. My advice to you, sir, is to remember always that the Company has your best interests in mind. The Company's purpose in all that is about to occur is simply to strengthen you for the tough battles that lie ahead in the world marketplace.

"The Company wants you to be a leader in those battles, otherwise you wouldn't be here. Remember, as you progress through the next phase, that obedience, loyalty, discipline, cooperation, and stoicism are the traits we seek to inculcate. These qualities will carry you to a high level of responsibility in the Company. And these qualities, developed by every employee in the Company, will assure the Company's ultimate success in the free marketplace. Thank you, and good luck!"

The MAS training facilities are a collection of smaller rooms, it appears, the first of which is a dining room similar in size and appointments to the room where I have been having dinner every night.

When I walk into this room, I am amazed to see my dinner companions — the hearty fellows who had joined me in drunken camaraderie last night. Only now they are looking very grim and unfriendly, sitting rigidly in the same order they are seated at dinnertime.

"Sit down," barks the big blond leader. "We're not talking here today. This is business, so keep quiet. This is a test of your loyalty to the group, not a test of your talent for carrying on meaningless conversations."

Two technicians enter carrying large, steaming cauldrons. They begin scooping giant helpings of a gray-looking substance onto the plates at the end of the table. A terrible odor fills the room, and I feel myself break out into a sweat.

When the technician fills my plate with the substance, I summon the courage to look at it. What I see is a horrible stewlike substance that resembles garbage. I stick my fork into the mess and stir it, uncovering a nightmarish brew of eggshells, coffee grounds, small bones, purplish spoiled meat, fish bones, and a stringy substance unlike anything I have seen before.

I manage a laugh. "This is pretty funny, you guys, but actually it makes me sick. Do we have to go on with this joke?"

"This is not a joke, you idiot," the blond leader shouts. "We are eating it, and you will too. If you don't, it's back to the machines with you — only this time we won't be playing."

I look around. My companions are eating it. They appear to be eating with gusto. I grow increasingly nauseated.

"What are you waiting for?" the blond leader screams at me. "You have been ordered to do something. Now do it."

I lift a forkful of the vile mess to my mouth, but I can hardly bring myself to taste it. Suddenly, from nowhere, my old nemesis from the first phase of the training — Carl, the master of the machines — appears and steps behind me. With both hands, he grabs my head and shoves my face into the plate.

"Eat. Eat," Carl commands in his old SS voice.

To my amazement, I begin eating the gruel. Each time I pause longer than Carl likes, he shoves my head back into the plate. None of this, I notice through tears of nausea, has any visible effect on my companions. Glancing around, I see that they are eating the gruel with apparent relish and have begun to carry on a conversation about some basketball game.

"Eat, eat," Carl keeps grunting. Suddenly, I can eat no more. Convulsed with nausea, I leap out of my chair and vomit on the man sitting at my left. The last thing I remember is the man's fist hurtling toward my face. Then everything goes black.

When I awake, I am sitting on the floor of a somewhat larger room. I am naked, and I notice my hands are still covered with some of my vomit. A huge technician is looming over me, his right hand holding a black leather whip.

"Enjoy your meal, did you? I hope so. Now, stand up," he shouts.

I drag myself to my feet. Suddenly, I feel the hot sting of the whip. Then again, and again.

"Discipline! Cooperation! Unity! Loyalty! Discipline! Cooperation! Unity! Loyalty! Come on, let's hear it from you," the trainer screams.

I can barely utter the words.

"Discipline," I murmur. "Cooperation. Unity. Loyalty. Cooperation. Unity. Loyalty."

"And conformity. Let's hear 'conformity,'" the trainer shrieks.

"Yes, yes, conformity," I whisper. "Discipline. Cooperation. Unity. Loyalty. Conformity. Conformity. Loyalty. Discipline. Unity." My voice trails off. But every time I falter, the whipping resumes until I begin to feel the blood running

down my back. Then the room begins to spin, the air turns
green and yellow and orange, and I slump onto the floor as
darkness surrounds me.

I revive to find a young female technician bathing me, carefully washing the blood from my back, the sponge sending
spasms of pain through my entire body.

"You'll be all right as soon as we get you dressed and you
have a few minutes' rest," the young woman says in a soothing voice. "You'll be glad to know that you're over the worst
part."

When the girl finishes bathing me, she hands me a clean
blue uniform to replace the jacket and slacks covered with
vomit that lie beside me on the floor.

"Put this on and take a few moments to catch your breath.
Another technician will be in momentarily to begin the next
part of the training," the girl says. Then she kisses me quickly
on the forehead and leaves.

Touching. A touch of Harriet in the night, I think. The
signal of tender concern before the final battle in which we
are all doomed to die. I put on the fresh uniform.

The door opens and a technician enters. It is the same
horn-rimmed fascist who gave me the introductory lecture at
the beginning of this phase.

Without a nod, his face frozen in the same lifeless expression he had worn before, he launches into another homily.

"Discipline in the battles of the free marketplace is not
measured merely by one's ability to endure pain, privation,
or suffering — to accomplish seemingly impossible tasks with
good cheer and grace," he begins in his preacher's voice.

"No, discipline and obedience are also measured by one's
ability, by one's willingness, to inflict pain on others, to overcome any feelings of affection, personal loyalty, or compas-
sion — to subordinate those feelings to the corporate goals
and to the corporate good."

He goes on at length in this fashion, his voice a steady drone without inflection, his sentences running together without punctuation. Finally, after ten minutes or so, he concludes his speech, asks me to wait a minute, and leaves the room.

I wait nervously, filled with dread at the prospect of this final, unthinkable conclusion to my long indoctrination in corporate leadership. What could be worse than what has already happened? I ask myself.

The door opens. Almost in lock step, my six dinner companions, who only a couple of hours ago had been swilling down the garbage that made me violently sick, march into the room, all completely naked.

The blond brute who always acts as leader stands in front of me, his face frozen in a mask of stoicism. Handing me a whip similar to the one just used on me, he says:

"Here. Take this and show your stuff. Give each of us a good beating. Don't worry about us. We can take anything you can dish out."

"But I can't do that," I say, my voice hardly audible. "You're my friends."

"You can and you will do that. If you don't, it's Carl and the machines again. Now get to it."

I grasp the whip in my right hand. As if performing some drill, the six hearty executives with whom I had shared dinner for the past two weeks turn their naked backs to me. I hesitate.

"Now!" the blond leader shrieks.

Stretching my arm as far behind me as I can, I lash the whip forward with a force that surprises me. The blond leader flinches, and blood begins oozing from three dark red bands on his upper back.

"Fantastic!" the blond leader screams. "Now again. And again! I want twelve of them, and then I want twelve for each of the others."

I ready the whip again, this time with a feeling of growing ease. It is not so bad, being a whipper. Better to be the whipper than the whipped, I think.

Again, a resounding blow to the blond leader's back, this time harder than the first. I think I hear him utter a low groan, but it could be my imagination.

Again and again I deliver the required lashes. The blood on the blond leader's back is now pouring down his body at an alarming rate. I feel sweat on my brow, and with each new blow, I know that I have "graduated" into the executive class, that all my suffering will pay off in money and perquisites that up to now have been unimaginable.

I don't know how many blows I deliver — perhaps as many as six — when all of a sudden nausea again overcomes me. My entire body is covered with sweat, the room begins to spin, and the vision of these six naked men waiting for the lash — my lash — fills me with a terror greater than I have ever known before.

Dropping the whip at my feet, I turn abruptly and run for the door. For a terrible moment, I have trouble turning the knob with my sweaty palm. Then it gives and I stumble into the corridor, slamming the door behind me.

I run down the corridor as fast as I can. The rush of the air against my face is the most pleasant sensation I have had in more than two weeks. The longer I run, the stronger I feel. Nausea gives way to an orgasmic sensation, the sensation of sudden freedom from a nightmare of humiliation and pain.

The corridor fills with a loud but pleasant sound of chimes and the sensual voice of a young woman announcing something. At first I can't make it out, but the chimes and the announcement keep repeating.

"The A team will please mobilize for condition Zebra," the young woman says. "The A team will please mobilize for condition Zebra."

As I try to run faster, I am struck by the thought that my

escape may be the first in the history of the Troubled Employee Department. If my escape succeeds, that is, for at that moment I see the giant body of a technician running toward me. As the distance closes, I recognize Carl.

With only a hundred feet or so to go before we collide, I come upon another corridor that branches to the right. With the grace of a gazelle eluding a lion, I turn into the new corridor just as Carl rushes past me, unable to stop in time.

Now I am running faster than I ever have in my life, confident that I can outdistance Carl. Finally I reach a door that I know leads into the reception room, where the cool blonde welcomed me a century ago. I fling myself against the door and rush past her, hearing Carl's shouts not far behind. One more door and I am in the tunnel that leads to the cafeteria where Conrad and I eat lunch.

Carl must be only a few steps behind me as I plunge headlong down the wide tunnel.

"Stop! Stop!" he shouts. "This man is a thief!"

The tunnel turns abruptly, and I am only a few yards from a group of secretaries carrying trays of coffee and soft drinks. I run right through them, knocking two of them down and scattering the drinks over the floor. I glance behind me just long enough to see Carl's huge frame sliding along toward the wall and rolling over the trays and cups.

In less than a minute I am outside the building, running through the vast parking lot. There is not a person in sight, which is typical for this time of day. The sun is bright, the sky a glorious deep blue, as I head for a large field bordering the parking lot. Panting and stumbling, I run through the field, glancing behind me every few seconds. Still, no one is to be seen.

In the distance, a subdivision of large mock colonial houses, one with a red garage door, appears faintly through the haze of heat. Although I have noticed this subdivision before —

one of a dozen like it in the immediate vicinity — I had not given it any thought, didn't know its name or what town it was in, and didn't care. But now it becomes my sanctuary, a place where my visit to hell could end.

As I continue to run, my pace slows, but my determination to reach these houses remains complete. I focus on the red garage door and keep going. I think of stopping to rest, but I know that the Company's security people and the local police are spreading out through the area right now in search of me. Just as I am about to collapse with exhaustion, I look up to see the house looming before me, its green lawn rippling gently in the warm breeze.

I plunge across the lawn, almost tripping over a small toy truck. I sprint across the driveway and pull the handle of the screen door. It is unlocked. I turn the doorknob and half fall into the cool interior. I am on a landing leading to the basement. I close the door softly and sit on one of the steps, gasping for air.

Footsteps approach. The door above me opens, and a young woman wearing faded jeans stands looking at me, her face white with fear.

"Who are you? What do you want?" she demands in a voice not altogether hostile.

"I need help," I answer, realizing instantly how stupid my reply must sound.

"Well, that's obvious. But what's happened to you? Look, you're exhausted. And what is that outfit you're wearing? It looks like a uniform. Are you an escaped convict? And what's that all over the uniform? Is that blood?"

"Look, lady, I can explain all this. Just let me get my breath."

A little girl of about three appears and grasps her mother's hand. Her face is a copy of her mother's, a beautiful little doll's face glazed with fright.

"Stay there. Please stay there and don't harm us. I want to get you a drink of water. I'll be back in a minute," the woman says.

"Lady, please," I beg. "I know you're going to call the police. Do me a favor, will you? I can explain later. Don't call the police. Call the FBI."

"The FBI? What will I tell them?"

"Tell them anything you want. Tell them your little girl's been kidnaped, if you want. Anything. Just don't call the local police."

The woman and her daughter disappear, closing the door behind them. I listen for her voice on the phone, but I can't make out the words. Sweat continues to pour from every part of my body. In the background, I imagine I can hear Carl's unmistakable voice. The stairway to the basement becomes dimmer and dimmer, and I feel my body slump onto the landing as the darkness returns.

25

MY FIRST VIEW of Saint Cecilia Mercy Hospital is the open door in front of my bed. The statue of a woman in robes with arms outstretched looms benevolently over the door frame. Still groggy, I believe for a minute that this is the same woman I had seen a few instants before at the head of the stairway, just before the door closed and darkness engulfed me. A nurse enters the room and leans over me, blocking the view of Our Lady of the Stairway.

"What is this place?"

"Saint Cecilia Mercy Hospital."

"What am I doing here? Who brought me here?"

"Just relax now, you need rest. A doctor will be here soon to answer your questions."

The nurse departs, and I am left to deal with these puzzles alone. I seem to remember little of anything, but as the minutes drag by, I begin to see first the long green corridor of the Troubled Employee Department, then the rows of grim machines, the dinners with my hearty colleagues, the grim walks with the prodding Rupert behind my back, and then a blank, followed by my running exhausted through an open field, barging into the quiet house in the subdivision next to headquarters, and my brief conversation with the young woman at the head of the stairway before tumbling to the landing and losing consciousness.

"This is Dr. Ramoviddi," the nurse announces at the doorway. A small dark man enters and approaches my bed briskly. He has a gentle smile and a manner that begins to put me at ease.

"Hello, how are you feeling today?" His accent is so heavy I can hardly understand him. "Are you feeling better, please?"

"I don't know. I don't know how I was feeling before."

"I see. Well, we are here to help you. Now tell me, what is your name?"

I tell him.

"And who is President of the United States?"

I answer to his satisfaction.

"And who am I?"

"You're a doctor."

"What kind of doctor?"

"I don't know."

"Well, I am a psychiatrist. I am here to help you, here to find out what your perceptions are about the immediate past, and to help you return to a normal life, your family, and your duties at the Company."

"I have no family."

"Well, then I suppose the Company will be serving as your family." Dr. Ramoviddi smiles. "Do you have any pain?"

"No."

Dr. Ramoviddi explains that I was taken to the hospital by the police, who received a call from a woman living in a subdivision only a short distance from my Company's headquarters. He goes on to say that such incidents are not unheard of. Sometimes an executive such as I, even a lower-ranking employee, will become confused, lose his sense of surroundings, and end up in a neighborhood nearby. It is not to be considered a genuine breakdown, Dr. Ramoviddi explains, only a reaction to excessive stress. Usually a few days' or a couple of weeks' rest in the hospital, combined with limited psychotherapy, will restore the victim of this kind of stress to complete health "so that you may return to your duties at the Company."

"I don't want to return to my duties at the Company," I retort.

"Of course you do, please." Dr. Ramoviddi smiles more warmly than before. "Now, you won't be saying that in just a few days. In just a few days, you will be back to normal and hardly able to wait to get back to your desk. Do you like activities? Do you like to bowl?"

"No."

"I want you to try bowling. Bowling is very relaxing. It is not hard to do, and it helps you regain a sense of effort and accomplishment, which is what you really need in the kind of state you are in now.

"Also, I am having you take some drugs that will help you relax and speed your return to the office. This is, of course, in the best interest of you and the Company."

"My God," I shout, "does everything have to be in the best interest of the Company? Do you actually work for the hospital or are you a company employee?"

"Of course, I work for the hospital." Dr. Ramoviddi smiles his most patient smile. "But I am not unsympathetic to the Company, its methods of organizing men and women in cooperative efforts, its objectives, and its excellent products. And I do feel it has a genuine concern for the health and happiness of its employees."

It is no use arguing. Dr. Ramoviddi is obviously one of them, either on the company payroll or the recipient of a handsome stipend paid like a bounty for each vagrant employee he returns to active duty.

"All right, all right," I say. "Whatever you want me to do. Just give me the drugs and the therapy and the bowling or whatever and get me out of here."

Dr. Ramoviddi nods and smiles. He is a very agreeable person, the rare kind of doctor who gives one the impression that he has a genuine, personal interest in each case. He tells me to get dressed and asks an attendant to show me the way to the bowling alley. He will see me at eight o'clock tonight in his office.

Dr. Ramoviddi's office is Spartan, too small even for a man of his size. But, as I look in the door, he appears to be perfectly content, smiling his warm, civilized smile as he signs some documents.

"Come in, come in," he commands cheerfully. "How did you enjoy your bowling, please?"

"It was all right, I guess."

"Still a bit depressed, eh? Well, we'll get you over that in short order. Now, sit down here in this chair and tell me everything you can recall about recent events."

Dr. Ramoviddi listens attentively but without comment as I recount the whole chain of events, leaving out nothing, including the last training sessions with the sadomasochistic whip exercises that caused me to flee.

Without showing any sign of impatience or disbelief, Dr. Ramoviddi smiles and sighs a long, mournful sigh.

"Well, now," he says softly. "Of course, we know none of that happened."

"What makes you say that?"

"Well, it does not match up with anything in our reservoir of experience or possibilities," he says.

"Just like that," I say. "Is that how you deal with such things? It isn't true because you say it couldn't happen? It doesn't fit the company definition of the possible?"

"Well, you have already told me about your earlier hallucinations, the flight of the pigeons and other episodes. So there is a precedent there. And we have no reason to think that these so-called events in the so-called Troubled Employee Department are anything more than an extension of your earlier hallucinations.

"But please, do not take offense. For you these visions, these sensations, have their own reality. A reality, I might say, more genuine than the reality that I seem to perceive.

"We are never at home. No, it is never easy, sorting out one man's version of reality from the version commonly accepted by the mass of mankind. It was Flaubert, I believe, who said, 'There is no truth, only perceptions.' So I am not without sympathy for your account of these recent events, not without understanding or even the willingness to believe. It is only my role as a physician that demands my rejection of these tales, that requires me to return you, as gently as possible, please, to the hard realities of the last few days. This is the essential step on the road to tranquillity. Perhaps there were green corridors, as you say, corridors in some part of the building that I am not familiar with. Perhaps even machines, some kind of exercise machines in a gymnasium tucked away in the basement. But there your accounting of your experience merges with fantasy and hallucination. We must work very hard, together, so that you can forget these nightmares and begin to see the visions of true events in your life before this most unfortunate episode occurred."

Dr. Ramoviddi says all this with a kind and philosophic voice, like a guru giving a novice instructions in some Oriental religion. The effect of his voice and manner is so reassuring that I don't answer him. I know, anyway, that argument is hopeless, that the treatment I am receiving here is only an extension of the training I escaped from in the Company's basement. And I know that the sooner I agree that my stories are only hallucinations, the sooner I will be able to return to a "normal" life.

"So, what do you think, please?" Dr. Ramoviddi asks.

"Well, I can't say I agree with you, but I will give it a try, work with you to see what this is all about."

"That is most cooperative, and we are pleased by your attitude. We will have two sessions a day. You will continue receiving the drugs during the coming days and perhaps experience a certain vertigo, an occasional sense of disorientation. But don't be alarmed. This is perfectly normal. I should also tell you that during this period you will begin to forget these stories that you have been relating to me, and the real events that took place during this period will begin to display themselves, as first light signals the beginning of a new day. And now, if you will excuse me, I will, please, make my way through the remainder of these forms."

26

I MIGHT HAVE EXPECTED Kreiznach would be out to check on me. If Room 111 really exists, as I am sure it does, my knowledge of it poses the most dangerous threat to the Company in its history. Thus it is no surprise that Kreiznach fidgets and squirms during his brief visit.

"Certainly you realize by now that this room you speak of — what is it, Room 111? — this room doesn't exist now, nor has it ever existed," Kreiznach assures me. "Surely Dr. Ramoviddi has succeeded in removing that illusion?"

"Let's say he has made me less certain than I was before," I reply. Although that is not at all true, I want him to feel I am making progress without pretending that I've experienced a miraculous cure.

"Well, that's good. I want you to know that we are all pulling for you, supporting you. It is not the first time this has happened. No, there was a case a few years ago of a man from Marketing who was found sitting on the median strip of a freeway about three miles from the office. This man had been under terrible stress from several directions, had the same kind of weird story you told, but eventually recovered very nicely and now laughs about the whole experience."

"Where is he now?"

"Somewhere in our European operations, I'm not exactly sure where. Anyway, the point is that a breakdown of the kind you experienced, if that's what we are calling it, is nothing to be ashamed of. It happens quite frequently and will not, I assure you, have the slightest impact on your career."

"I find that a little hard to believe."

"Well, believe me. Just believe me, that's all I ask. Look, I've got to be going now. A couple of reports to get out of the way before the weekend. We'll have you out of here and back to work in no time at all. Take care. See you later."

Kreiznach's departure is nervous and abrupt. I know he is under a lot of pressure to make sure that my return to head-quarters goes smoothly. Any hint of where I have spent the last few weeks, or any suggestion that I have an interesting tale to tell about the Company's Troubled Employee Department, could spell disaster for him — the end of his career.

When I awake the next day, I am startled by the realization that everything that happened to me in the Troubled Employee Department is only an illusion. How do I know this? I can't answer that. I struggle mightily with this new thought, but I can't shake it. It is like waking from a dream believing that the dream really happened. Yet I know now that all of these memories of Room 111 and my escape are pure fantasy. The idea occurs to me that this epiphany is all too convenient to be genuine; it fits nicely into the Company's plans and saves me a lot of embarrassment and trouble. Yet, try as I may, I can't deny this new truth — that everything I so firmly believed in only yesterday is now nothing more than a fairy tale.

Giddy with relief, I dress hurriedly and rush down the hallway to Dr. Ramoviddi's office. I try the door and find it locked. A nurse tells me that Dr. Ramoviddi won't be in his office until nine. Two hours. What should I do? I walk down the stairs to the bowling alley and try the door. It is open, so I walk in. There are no pins standing, no balls visible. I sit down in one of the chrome and plastic chairs. Nothing to do. Nothing to do but wait until nine o'clock and think about things. Maybe if I think long enough, the pendulum will swing back and I can return to my more comfortable mode — believing in Room 111 and all that happened there.

The time goes slowly, and I use it to review every detail of my elaborate fantasy. Every sight, every sound, every smell, pain, and taste of that long nightmare is clear and authentic. The parts of the puzzle are there without question, but when I put them all together, the puzzle itself looks false and unreal. I switch back and forth in a crazy rhythm. It happened. It didn't happen. But the "happened" motif fades, and by the time I notice that it's nine o'clock, I'm back to believing that it was all a fantasy.

Elated that my new opinion has withstood such a severe test, I rush back upstairs to Dr. Ramoviddi's office.

"Come in, come in, you're looking better." He smiles between gulps of coffee.

I rush into the room and blurt out that I have come over to his opinion. I now know without any shadow of doubt that the whole outlandish story I told him was nothing but fantasy, the product of a baroque imagination working in a mind that was half crippled by stress.

"Excellent, excellent!" Dr. Ramoviddi says, so excited that he spills his coffee over the papers on his desk. "The only thing that surprises me is that you came around so quickly. Usually these things take a little longer. We try to stretch them out a little to prevent false recoveries that can lead to a severe setback. You are certain, please, that you now believe this honestly, that you will never again revert to your original belief in the existence of Room 111?"

I think it is a curious question, but I don't have any trouble answering it. For one thing, I know what the answer is. For another, I know that a positive reply is my ticket out of this hospital.

"Certainly, yes, of course," I answer redundantly.

"Good! I have been aware for some time that this aberration of yours has been fading. So we see what a little rest, a little recreation, a little reflection, and the support of your company friends can do. I am sending you back tomorrow. Come back later this afternoon, fill out some forms, and you can begin packing."

Walking back to my room, I have a feeling of exhilaration. I will be free again. Even the dullness of the corporate environment seems pleasant. It will be good to see Conrad again and tell him about these crazy events. Of course, I will never suggest that Room 111 was anything but an illusion. Conrad will consider it all hilarious. He will want every detail of my stay in the hospital. He will want to know all about Kreiznach's visit and what kind of reception I get from Marlott on my return. Oh, there will be papers to shuffle, stupid speeches to write, dull meetings to attend. But as I scurry around my tiny room, packing my few belongings, I realize I can hardly wait until morning.

27

MARLOTT DOESN'T MENTION my absence. He behaves as if I had never left his office, as if there had been only a short pause while he answered the telephone. He is very friendly, unnaturally so, and I wonder if all of this is part of a company program worked out to make my return as smooth as possible.

None of my coworkers takes the slightest notice of my absence, either. They, too, are unnaturally friendly, or so I imagine. It seems as if everything has been frozen in time, exactly as I left it, except for an almost imperceptible shift in shading, with brighter tones throughout. Everything seems more cheerful, everything seems more orderly, all of it seems to make more sense. A distinctly tranquil ambience fills the corridors and offices, and I find myself walking through the building that I once despised with a new feeling of peace.

I plunge into my work with unprecedented vigor. Since my return, I am struck with the glowing congeniality of my col-

leagues. Barbara Burdoch seems more friendly and cooperative than before. No longer do I confront her with a feeling of
dread and suspicion. My assignments seem challenging and
sensible, whereas I once approached them with fear and
hatred. In meetings, I find myself filled with ideas, and I
express them with force and eloquence. People begin to con-
gratulate me on my "contributions." They do not suggest that
I have changed for the better, but I can see from their attitude that they think I have undergone some kind of transformation. All this leaves me with the thought that perhaps
the treatment at Saint Cecilia's involved something more than
the drugs and the meetings with Dr. Ramoviddi. Was there
a lobotomy? Shock treatment? Some kind of experimental
drug that will cause me to suffer some horrible side effects?
I put all this aside. I know I have suffered too long. First
through my own negative attitude toward the Company, then
through the trauma of my breakdown, and finally during the
period of treatment, when I had to make my way back to
reality.

I work very hard on the Chairman's "The Future Is Tomorrow" speech. He coined the phrase himself, and while I
first greeted it with skepticism, I now find myself feeling that
it has a certain catchiness and subtle depth. In any event, the
Chairman is quite proud of it, and I try to work it into the
speech as often as possible.

There are numerous meetings in connection with this
speech, which is to be given in three weeks to a national convention of land surveyors. I am not quite certain why the
Chairman is speaking to these surveyors; they haven't even
the most remote connection to our business. But there is great
excitement because we succeeded in getting this "platform"
for the Chairman, and everybody is pitching in to make it a
genuine success. We have bought twelve tables for various
dignitaries from the area, and we have been issuing periodic

press releases that promise the speech will contain important news.

What this important news will be has so far not been revealed even to me, but Marlott and others keep hinting that I will not be disappointed. Evidently, some of my colleagues have been let in on the secret, because whenever there is a meeting on the subject of the speech, there are winks and significant looks when the subject of the so far secret news is mentioned.

The Art Department is working hard on a collection of props reflecting the "Future Is Tomorrow" theme. There are also to be various media presentations — slides, movies, music, and even a troupe of mimes. All of this takes elaborate planning and coordination, which in turn require an extraordinary number of meetings. It is in these meetings that my new personality makes its startling debut. It is as if I had the same mind but a different body. But of course my mind is not the same, either, since my whole reaction to the people and to the work is entirely positive.

The dress rehearsal for the Chairman's "future" speech is something of a triumph. Everything has been rehearsed so many times, everyone is so sure of his role, that most of our earlier tension has disappeared. Even Marlott is in a relaxed mood, knowing that the Chairman is enthusiastic about the speech. It doesn't really matter what the audience or the press will think, because the only critic who counts has already given his approval.

The Chairman looks very competent in his dark gray pinstripe with the maroon tie and its matching handkerchief. He smiles broadly as he takes his place on the podium and gazes out at the twenty or so people who have been working on the speech and its presentation.

He clears his voice a bit nervously.

"Of course, at the beginning, I'm going to have a couple of

topical jokes to get things off to a good start," he announces somewhat shyly. "I understand some of you people are developing some material for me that will be appropriate."

"That's right, sir," Marlott shouts from the back of the room. "We'll have that for you tomorrow."

"Okay, then let's begin," the Chairman says.

The lights dim, and the drapes at the rear of the stage roll back, revealing a huge triptych of a screen. The room is filled with rock music, and the screens are filled with a light show, strange shapes and forms resembling amoebas, shifting and changing abruptly in time with the music.

The Chairman begins reading from his invisible Tele-PrompTer, giving the impression that he has memorized this forty-five-minute speech.

"What message do I have for you folks today? It is a message of importance, a message for history, a message written on the wind, a message carried on the soul of humanity through eons of history. The message is hope, the hope of mankind, the thing that keeps each and every one of us going, the thing that provides the fuel of progress for Spaceship Earth. What is this message? It is a simple message. A timely one. A timeless one. It is simply this: the future is tomorrow."

The Chairman steps back from the podium, turns halfway around, and looks up at the screen. The music blasts forth again, and the company name fills each of the screens in a variety of type styles and colors, dancing, expanding, contracting, blinking, exploding. The Chairman watches this with a transfixed expression.

When the music fades and the images on the screens disappear, the Chairman steps back to the podium and resumes his speech.

"We emerged from World War Two as the most powerful nation on earth, the envy of the world, the hope of mankind. For years we enjoyed this position, but now we are facing the greatest test we have faced since Washington battled the terrible winter of Valley Forge."

The Chairman drones on, and I begin to feel uneasy. The speech has gone through twenty-two drafts, and in its present form represents "input" from no fewer than sixty-four people, including people from Marketing, Legal, Finance, Engineering, Advertising, Accounting, and Security. Through all of this, I am struck by occasional negative thoughts, even thinking at one point that the speech is pure nonsense, a failed imitation of Edward Lear. I remember stopping in to see Conrad once and finding him in an ecstasy of frustration, the pages of his latest rejected draft lying on the floor. Conrad had put a fresh sheet of paper in his typewriter, put a number 1 at the top, and typed "Ladies and gentlemen."

"What now? What the hell do I write now?" he asked me, his face distorted with frustration. "Wait! I got it!" He began typing furiously.

I walked around behind his chair and looked down. Conrad was typing "doodah" over and over again.

"That's it!" Conrad shouted as I left the room quietly. "Doodah. Doodah. Doodah. That'll satisfy them! How can they quarrel with that? Who's going to dispute the truth, the essential wisdom of 'doodah'?"

I think of this as I watch the Chairman deliver the words I have struggled so long to produce. I know that even if I wanted to, I couldn't take credit for these words, because they aren't mine. Nor are they anybody's. The words, of course, are meaningless, and the speech is utterly without substance. But none of that is important. The important thing is that the Chairman of one of the largest corporations in the country will be standing up before a thousand land surveyors, their wives, and girlfriends, uttering various slogans and "thoughts" between outbursts of music and bright images exploding on three oversize screens. Surely the very appearance of this important man will inspire everyone in the audience. Surely some of his wisdom, his power, his competence, will flow out to every corner of the room, and everyone there will leave the room more powerful, more competent, more understanding of the problems of the free marketplace than they were when they arrived. The whole event will be a combination revival meeting, political convention, rock concert, and dinner theater — a ritual not easily dismissed or soon forgotten.

The Chairman stops talking. The music stops, the screens go blank, and the room is suddenly quiet. The Chairman, smiling ecstatically, stands at the podium, wiping his brow with the maroon handkerchief. No one says a word.

From the back of the room comes a deep sigh, a sigh of disbelieving admiration, a sigh that sounds as if it had been rehearsed for hours.

"Sir? Sir?" It is Marlott.

"Yes?" the Chairman asks expectantly, leaning slightly forward against the podium.

"That is simply the greatest speech that was ever given in this country. Simply the greatest, and I'm not kidding."

"Thank you. Thank you so much. I thank each and every one of you here today who has helped make this speech such a success."

People begin shaking hands. Workers appear from the wings of the stage and shake hands with us. People grab Marlott and pat him on the back. From a door at the side of the auditorium, the projectionist emerges. A man in his sixties, he has worked hundreds of speeches and presentations. He is the Chairman's favorite, because no one can remember that he has ever made a mistake. The man is trembling, sweating, and he is the only person in the room who is not smiling. Marlott walks over, grabs his hand, and shakes it vigorously.

"Listen!" Marlott shouts. "Everybody listen! Without this man, without Kocinski, none of this could ever have happened. You can't have a good speech without a good projectionist, and this one — this Kocinski — is the greatest projectionist in the world!"

Everybody applauds. The Chairman nods his smiling approval, and an assistant picks up his briefcase. The Chairman waves to all of us, steps down from the stage, and goes out the side door.

Marlott pats me on the back on the way out.

"Great job. Great job. Might as well tell you now. You're up for promotion!"

28

I FIND IT HARD to believe that I'm on my way to the thirty-second floor to attend a meeting of something called the Interim Strategic Planning and Operational Committee. In the first place, I have never heard of this committee, which is not especially surprising in itself, considering the number of obscure committees that I know exist. What is surprising is that I have been invited to attend the meeting of a group important enough to assemble on the thirty-second floor. In telling me to attend, Marlott could hardly conceal his pleasure, smiling all the time, winking, and clearing his throat significantly. Apparently he considered it a major breakthrough for me. So as I make my way past the security people and down the corridor of the thirty-second floor, I am full of apprehension and excitement.

The door to the conference room is closed. Perhaps I am late. I gently push the door open and make my way in, trying to be as inconspicuous as possible. The meeting is already under way, and I look at my watch in annoyance. It has stopped. At first I am too embarrassed to look around the room. When I do, I receive a shock that almost knocks me out of my seat. The six men sitting around the room are my dinner companions from the Troubled Employee Department, the same men whose naked bodies I had declined to whip!

I must be mistaken. This can't be. If this is true, it means that the pact I have made with myself, to bury forever the fantasy of my weeks behind the door of Room 111, is destroyed. It means the revival of terrible memories that I have succeeded in dismissing. It forces upon me the awful task of reconciling those preposterous memories with the accepted boundaries of reality. Worst of all, it would force me to act, to expose the whole sadistic corporate apparatus to the entire world.

Yet I am not mistaken. The chairman of this committee is the big, deep-throated athletic blond who seemed to be the group's unofficial leader in Room 111. And there's the one with the scar on his left cheek. And the sincere one who told dirty jokes without smiling. Every one of them is part of the same nightly cast that helped shape me into someone socially fit to join the executive class.

"Why don't you pull your chair up to the table and join us. You really haven't missed anything. We're just starting," says the blond leader.

My palms turn sweaty, and I feel the blood rushing to my head as I comply. But suddenly I feel something inside me take over, as if an inner switch has been pulled. As I settle into my chair, I find myself coolly surveying every face at the table. Almost unconsciously, I realize that my mouth is fixed in the same semismile that used to fill me with such contempt when I saw it on the faces of my coworkers as they strode along the corridors. But now, without thinking about it, I have assumed the same supercilious expression. And, as I adjust the papers in front of me, I announce in the most astounding basso profundo:

"I would have been here on time, but I had a meeting of the Global Logistics Committee in another building."

No one responds, but I know they are impressed. A curious expression overtakes the chairman's face, but he goes on with what he was saying as if nothing had happened. The meeting takes the usual course — a series of presentations with elaborate charts, slides, and movies; a general discussion in which each participant politely ignores whatever the previous speaker has said; various anecdotes and jokes with no relevance to the subject being discussed. To my own surprise, I find myself doing a lot of talking. It surprises me further that my near-dominance of the meeting, far from offending the group, seems to please them. Several of them comment favorably on what I say, and one of them passes me a note that says, "Your comments are both constructive and eloquent. Right on!"

Just as the meeting is about to end, I clear my throat and launch into a summary that lasts a good ten minutes. I review the competitive scene in our principal markets, give an overview of the currency exchange problem and its probable course for the balance of the year, comment lengthily on the theoretical distinctions between quality and perceived quality, describe a recent article I read on technology transfer, and end with an upbeat plea for a new, company-wide effort to develop an effective instrument for long-range strategic planning.

When I finish, there is a profound silence, and I wonder if I have overstepped the limits of executive propriety. But to my relief the group bursts into a long round of applause, and the group leader gives me a mock salute.

"Well done, well done," he intones. "It's the kind of leadership you showed here today that's the key to this Company's progress in the next decade. We're darned glad to have you aboard this committee, because there's going to be some rough sailing ahead. We need all the navigation we can get, and it sure looks like you've got your bearings."

The group gathers up its papers and files out of the room. One of the men comes up to me and says:

"Hey! How'd you like a couple of tickets to tonight's game. Box seats. It's a double-header, too."

"Hey, thanks a lot. Sure, I'll take them." I give him a big pat on the back, and we head on down the corridor, two deadly rivals in temporary alliance.

29

NOW I AM IN THE worst conflict of my life, an internal conflict that threatens to force me back into Saint Cecilia's. The encounter with my Room 111 dinner companions in the thirty-second-floor conference room confirms the existence of the Troubled Employee Department. This in turn will certainly force me to take action to expose the whole outrageous program. And yet the stunning fact is that the training program that takes place in Room 111 transformed me completely, from a hesitant, unsure, resentful follower who was losing ground in his career to a dynamic, forceful, deep-voiced, optimistic superexecutive who is suddenly cutting a wide path through the Company's higher echelons. Was I to abandon this sudden status, give up my new success entirely, to fight some ridiculous battle aimed at exposing a cruel and bizarre executive training program that broke men and sent them to a mental hospital? Who would believe me, anyway, given the Company's enormous resources to lie, conceal, and explain?

It would be a fight I couldn't win for a victory not worth having. On the other hand, could I really live with myself, knowing that lesser men than I who followed me to the Troubled Employee Department might be completely destroyed by the experience?

Conrad isn't any help in all of this. He, too, has undergone a complete transformation, at least in his relationship with me. No more the funny cynical comments, no more the excited wry accounts about the latest outrage. Instead he has become withdrawn, avoiding me at all costs, and sullen and suspicious when he is forced into contact with me.

"Look," he says when I press him to talk, "I don't want to get into any of this. I don't know anything about a Troubled Employee Department, so I don't really feel I have anything to contribute. Anyway, you seem to be getting along just fine lately, so why worry about it?"

I give up on Conrad. Too bad, but I really don't need him anymore. I find myself avoiding him, and when his name is mentioned among my new friends, I remain silent. It is good strategy; I am not really criticizing him. I am just acting as if he doesn't exist.

But my dilemma grows worse. The memory of the machines grows more and more vivid, and I wake up at night from dreams in which I hear the vivid, profane shouts of Rupert just a few feet behind me.

One day something happens that forces me to take action. I am on my way to a meeting on the thirty-second floor when the elevator stops at the tenth floor. The door opens, and Carl walks in. There is no mistake about it. It is Carl — the same cruel mouth, the same boxer hands, the same huge shoulders. He is not wearing the blue uniform of Room 111 trainers. He is wearing a gray flannel suit, which looks slightly ridiculous on his wrestler's frame. He appears not to recognize me and turns his back on me the instant he steps in. My heart goes crazy, and my whole body fills with rage. I want to kick him in the small of his back, break his back, then crush his face under my heels. But I do nothing. We are only in the elevator for a few seconds, but it is long enough for me to construct elaborate fantasies about killing the man who stands unaware of me only inches away.

The encounter with Carl is so frightening that I decide to skip the meeting. I hurry back to the office and have my secretary call the committee secretary and make excuses. Then I close the door and try to think. Why not forget it, just forget it? So what if I saw Carl on the elevator? He didn't seem to notice. So what if the people on the Strategic Planning Committee turned out to be my social instructors in Room 111? The main thing is that I have achieved an important breakthrough. Marlott is already hinting about still another promotion only a few weeks after my first promotion in seven years. My momentum is phenomenal. The future, as the Chairman put it, is tomorrow. I could end up a vice president within a year or so, given what has happened in the last month.

All this is true, but it is not enough. The whir of the machines in Room 111 fills my ears, and my body surges with the sharp remembered pain.

I leap out of my chair and fly out the door, rush down the hall to the elevator, and down the elevator to the basement. I dash through the long tunnel, sliding and nearly falling, glancing at the numbers along the way. Room 87, 89, 91, 93 — they rush by me in a haze of excitement. Room 105, 107, 109, 113. What happened to Room 111? There is no Room 111. I look at the other side of the corridor. Room 106, 108, 110, 112. No, it wouldn't be there, anyway.

But if there is no Room 111, and there is certainly none with that number, why not? The absence of a Room 111 is every bit as significant as if I had found it there. But if no room has the number I'm looking for, I can't try the knob, burst in, and find the blond secretary sitting there exactly where I discovered her only a few weeks ago.

I try the rooms on each side of the tunnel. I try the rooms on both sides of the place where Room 111 should be. But they are all locked. I study the labels on the door. They are all meaningless. Central American Transportation Studies. North American Product Evaluation. Advanced Reconciliation and Adaptation Research. Names like these.

Someone comes toward me through the tunnel. I can't be seen trying doorknobs. I turn and walk slowly back toward the elevator. A fat man in his shirtsleeves carrying a stack of papers passes me.

"Excuse me, sir."

"Certainly."

I'm depressed as the elevator takes me back to my floor. It is time to see Dr. Mirsch again.

30

"WHAT'S ON YOUR MIND today?" Dr. Mirsch asks, his mouth full of chocolate chip cookies from a bag on his lap. He has gained at least ten pounds since I last saw him.

"Plenty. Stuff you wouldn't believe. Stuff that makes the pigeons look tame. But this stuff is real. I know you won't believe it, but it all actually happened."

Dr. Mirsch says nothing. I could cram the cookies, bag and all, down his throat, so furious am I at his detachment.

"Okay. Here goes. But I don't want to hear you ask, 'How do you feel about this?' "

I tell him the whole story. When I am finished, I look at my watch. Only five minutes of my session remain. Dr. Mirsch is silent.

"Well?" I demand, turning around to face him.

"What are your thoughts about this?"

"Goddamn it!" I shout. "What are *your* thoughts?"

He doesn't answer.

"Do you think it's another hallucination?"

"We can't be certain about these things, can we? Look, let's go into this more deeply later. Our time is up today."

Driving back to the office, it occurs to me that it's the same old story: a conspiracy of silence or denial in the face of my clear and detailed accounts. A conspiracy that very possibly involves Dr. Mirsch himself, knowing as I do that many of his patients work for the Company. Has he been paid off to keep quiet? Does he really believe that the whole story, rich in detail, is a product of my imagination? Does he really believe that the gradually healing welts on my back that I showed him, midway in the session, were received in some sado-masochistic orgy I attended on my own time?

One thing I can do, I decide, is to go back to the house in the subdivision, talk to the woman who found me on the stairway, and see if I can pick up any clues that might help prove that this all really happened.

I drive to the subdivision, make my way through the maze of streets, and, after a couple of false starts, find the house with the unmistakable red garage door that served as a distant beacon while I ran exhausted through the field that hot day.

I park the car in the driveway and ring the bell.

The woman appears at the door. The same woman, without mistake. The same beautiful brown hair, upturned nose, and pale blue eyes full of sympathy and understanding.

"Yes?" she asks in a slightly apprehensive voice.

"Don't you remember me?"

"I'm afraid not. Why should I?" She is not so friendly as I have imagined her.

"From the stairway. Just a few weeks ago, a very hot day it was. You found me on the stairway. Had a breakdown or something. You called the police."

"Oh, sure. Now I remember. I'm sorry, it's just that you

were wearing something different that day and I didn't recognize you. Besides, you were exhausted and quite a bit
thinner. Are you feeling better now?"

She isn't going to let me in. I see her push the lock on the
screen door.

"Well, yes. Quite a bit. Look, I know you're busy, but I
want to ask you a couple of questions. Do you have time?"

"I guess so. A couple of minutes, anyway."

"What was I wearing that day?"

"Some kind of uniform. I thought you were a garage mechanic or something. It was blue, like a mechanic's, maybe,
but it was quite clean, as I recall."

"What did I say?"

"I don't remember that you said much of anything. You
were very, very tired, because you had been running a long
way. I guess you did ask for a drink of water. But I had to
call the police, you know. You just can't take chances with
some stranger barging into your house like that. I'm sorry,
but I had to."

"Did you notice anything else about me?"

"Yes, I did, as a matter of fact. Fear. You looked terribly
afraid of something. Your eyes were full of terror. I knew
something horrible had just happened to you, and that made
me even more frightened."

"And you called the police?"

"Yes, but they didn't actually come."

"They didn't come? What do you mean? Who did come?"

"Well, it was the security people from your own Company.
They seemed to know all about you and said that you had
been working in one of the laboratories when you seemed to
have a seizure of some kind and just ran out of the building.
They identified themselves, had company uniforms on and
everything. I hope I didn't do anything wrong. It all seemed
all right to me, and they assured me that they would take you
right to the hospital."

"I see. And they took me away in their own car?"

"Yes."

"Did you ever hear anything else from anyone at the Company?"

"Mmmmm. Well, yes. Yes, I did, come to think of it. A doctor called. Can't remember his name. Italian name, it seems to me. Music. Oh, that's it! Dr. Mancini."

"Dr. Mangones."

"That's it. Dr. Mangones."

"Well, what did he say?"

"Oh, nothing very much. He was very nice. He thanked me for looking after you, and he asked me not to talk about this, because naturally it would be embarrassing to you if word got around that you had had this breakdown. I guess not many people in your department knew what had happened. They just thought you got violently sick and went to the bathroom."

The woman starts fussing with the door latch, and I can tell she wants me to leave.

"Listen, I do want to thank you for taking such good care of me that day. I know it must have been a frightening experience for you, and I'm glad you were able to do the right thing and call the police without fainting or something."

"Well, that's okay. Look, I've got to go now. Take care of yourself."

"Okay. And once more, thanks."

The visit to the subdivision confirms what I already know, that there is a house where I sat on the landing in a blue uniform, exhausted and terrified. And there is a Dr. Mangones, as I knew all along. But beyond that, the heart of the mystery remains intact. Why is there no evidence of a Room 111? How can an establishment as extensive as the Troubled Employee Department, with dozens of employees, a huge area, and all of its elaborate equipment, how can this entire department disappear without a trace in such a short period of time?

I drive back to the office more disturbed than ever. In confirming my sanity, I have also proven the mendacity of everyone in the Company, dozens of people who know about the Troubled Employee Department but deny its existence. What will I do now? Will there be more sleepless nights, more nightmares about the machines, about Dr. Mangones and Carl and Rupert? Why did I revive the mystery by trying to find Room 111 and visiting the woman in the subdivision? It is all pushing me over the brink, this time for real, and Dr. Mirsch is no help at all.

31

MY PROMOTION TO vice president, public affairs, comes as
a thunderbolt. The fact that I jump over six people above me
is only part of it. The way it is done is unprecedented in the
Company's history. A surprise call to the Chairman's office.
A smiling Chairman shaking my hand, giving me a little
speech of welcome and congratulations. Marlott standing by,
trying to smile, and the Chairman asking him to fix us a
drink. Drink in hand, he chats with me as if I'm nearly an
equal.

"You know, frankly, on that trip to Los Angeles you didn't
make much of an impression on me," the Chairman says.
"But I've been getting outstanding reports on your progress
in the last few weeks and I'm very impressed. We looked at
all the evidence, looked at the candidates, and when we finished, there was no question in our mind that you were our
man.

"Incidentally, you did one hell of a job on my 'Future Is
Tomorrow' speech. That speech got a lot of positive reaction,

and while the way I delivered it might have had something to do with that, it was the way you wrote it that really counted."

"Thanks very much, sir. I appreciate that. Incidentally, sir, I want to say that delivery is really far more important in determining the success of a speech than the content itself."

"Well, I don't know about that. But I do know that together we make a pretty good team. Marlott, why don't you get us all another drink?"

I know Marlott is probably furious, but he covers it up pretty well. I am up there at least half an hour, and when I get back and word gets around about what has happened and how it happened, there are a lot of astonished faces on my floor, faces that are also suddenly far friendlier than I have ever seen them before.

Now I am sitting in my new office on the thirty-second floor, just three offices down from the Chairman, wondering whether this unbelievable turn of fortune will end my determination to solve the mystery of Room 111. The office is huge, full of wood paneling, with automatic drapes, the largest credenza I have ever seen, and two original Matisses on the walls. It is everything any careerist could ever want, yet having it all doesn't cure my uneasiness. Perhaps it's the way I got here that reduces my pleasure. Which means that I have still not laid to rest the disturbing memories of Room 111. True, they don't wake me up at night anymore, but at times like this, when my thoughts should be on work, on the joy of winning, those memories intrude.

There is only one person who can help me, as much as I dislike him. Dr. Mirsch. But if I put the question to him, he would only ask, "What do you think?"

Anyway, the important thing isn't to confirm the existence of the Troubled Employee Department or to convince myself once and for all that it was all a hallucination. No. The important thing is to resolve the whole situation in the least troublesome way, to arrive somehow at the conclusion that even if Room 111 does exist, it would be better for me and everybody involved just to forget about it.

But a chance encounter with Conrad prevents a quiet, clean resolution. I am on my way to a meeting on my old floor when I see him, looking, in the distance, exactly like Conrad — somewhat frayed, slightly depressed, and a bit sullen. But as I get closer, I see that Conrad is troubled and excited about something.

"Say," he begins in a slightly strained voice, "didn't you say all that Troubled Employee Department stuff took place in Room 111?"

"I did."

"But I thought you said you went down there and couldn't find a room with that number."

"I did say that."

"Well, I was just down there, and there is a door with 111 on it."

"You're kidding."

"No, I'm not. Go see for yourself."

I do just that, moving as fast as the decorum of my new title allows. As I hurry through the long tunnel, I slow my pace as I get closer to where the room should be, not wanting to attract any more attention than necessary to the presence of a vice president in the basement.

There it is, just as Conrad said it would be: Room 111: Latin American Operations and Planning.

Cautiously, I turn the doorknob, and to my amazement the door springs open. Inside, I find the reception room looking the same as I remember it, except that no one is behind the desk. A smoking cigarette butt indicates the receptionist was there only a minute ago. I may have time to get to the corridor that leads from the door just behind her desk. I make a

dash for it. Success. I close the door softly and walk as non-
chalantly as I can along a hallway I remember all too well. I
turn and continue along another corridor toward the Trainorium. I am in luck; except for me, the halls are empty. My
heart pounding, I slowly open the door labeled Trainorium
and peek inside. It is all there — the gleaming machines, the
loudspeakers, the burly trainer, and a poor trainee in a blue
uniform stretched out on Machine Number 3.

I close the door as gently as I opened it, but not before I
hear a piercing shriek that fills the entire room. As quickly
as I can, I retrace my steps to the receptionist's office. I pause,
knowing that the next move could be fatal. It is now or never.
I push the door open and walk quickly inside. Empty. I hurry
on through the room and into the tunnel outside. Again —
fabulous luck — not a soul in sight. Wiping my brow, I
breathe more easily and walk quickly to the elevator. Back in
my office, I ask my secretary not to disturb me and close the
door. What now? Truth is very untidy, very troublesome.
Better by far to continue with the illusion that everything
was a fantasy. But the truth can't be controlled; now it con-
trols me.

So it's back to Dr. Mirsch, the final arbiter of reality, de-
stroyer of dreams, sworn enemy of illusion.

"Look, Dr. Mirsch, today I want something different," I
begin, my body stiff with anger and impatience. "Today I
want answers — not ambiguities, not palliatives, not mind
cookies. Today I want the truth, and if you can't give me the
truth, I'll give it to you."

Even Dr. Imperturbable seems shaken by this aggressive
beginning. His voice breaks slightly:

"Why are you making threats against me?"

"Because I'm tired of playing around with this. The fact is
that I have seen the past, and it's behind a door marked 111."

"What do you mean, you've seen the past?"

"Just what I said. I have seen Room 111, opened the door, gone in, walked through the reception room, down the corridors, and looked in on the Trainorium, where I suffered so terribly to become the superexecutive that I am today. I have seen it all. Saw it all yesterday just as it existed two months ago. What do you say to that? Or, as you would put it, how do you feel about that?"

I can feel the anger well up so quickly that it threatens to choke me, to cut off my breath.

"I feel that we have a lot of work to do," Dr. Mirsch replies with his usual voice of cool professionalism.

It is too much. All of my suffering in Room 111, the misery of Saint Cecilia's, the excitement and guilt of my promotion to vice president, and my rage at Dr. Mirsch's neutrality combine in an explosion of emotion.

I leap from the couch and grab the startled doctor by the collar.

"Get up!" I scream. "Get your fat ass off that chair and come with me. And leave your cookies behind."

"All right, all right. No need to get violent. I'll be happy to go with you. Do you know at this point where you are going?"

Dr. Mirsch's infuriating calm destroys my capacity to speak. Shoving, poking, pulling, I lead him out to my car, guide him into the passenger seat, jump behind the wheel, and drive off with squealing tires.

It is Saturday afternoon, and the streets are busy with people on their way to the hardware store. We make our way slowly down the long thoroughfare, turn once, and drive three miles through a neighborhood of middle-class homes to the huge tract of neatly manicured grass dominated by the black monolith that is the Company's headquarters.

I park in the vice-presidential lot, mercifully close to the entrance, and usher the silent Dr. Mirsch through the door.

"Would you please sign the log, sir?" the guard asks, smiling pleasantly.

Without a word, I sign the log and escort Dr. Mirsch past the desk to an open elevator. It is a good time to perform this task, because only a handful of people are in the building. We get in the elevator and I push the button for the basement. The elevator moves silently and swiftly, the door opens, and we step into the long, deserted tunnel.

"This is kind of crazy." Dr. Mirsch chuckles. "It is not how it should have been done, but it seems to be your way, doesn't it?"

"You bet."

We encounter no one in the corridor. We come to the door marked 111, and I shove it open without pausing. I push Mirsch through the door and feel the thrill of vindication. The reception room is exactly as it should be — nothing changed. No one is there, and I remember that there is no receptionist on duty during the weekend. I hurry to the inner door and find it locked. Panicked, I pound on it with my fist. When no one comes, I resume pounding. My fist is starting to hurt badly when I finally hear the lock turning. The door opens abruptly, and there stands the enormous figure of Carl, a particularly ominous expression on his face.

I react instinctively with a solid kick to Carl's groin, and he doubles over with a terrible shriek. My right knee smashes up into his face, and as he slumps to the floor, I see drops of blood hit the green vinyl floor. Dr. Mirsch lets out a short, frightened sigh.

"Come on, let's go!" I shout, hurrying him along with a push.

We rush off down the corridor, doctor and patient, although this time I am the doctor and Dr. Mirsch is the patient. The roles are reversed, I am thinking, because Dr. Mirsch himself has been leading a life of illusion, surrounded by his own little fantasy world of fat insurance fees, compliant, respectful patients, and the solid support of the corporate hierarchy in his efforts to get his patients back to their offices as soon as possible. The real world is here, at the end of this long green corridor where corporate America trains its warriors to do battle against the tough little Japanese, the current champions of the world marketplace.

So I think as I half lead, half push, Dr. Mirsch toward the door at the very end of this corridor, the door I fled through in terror only two months ago.

When we reach the door I am covered with sweat, and Dr. Mirsch has an expression of bemused terror on his face.

I fling the door open and push the doctor a couple of feet ahead of me. Looking over his shoulder, I see the whole scene just as I had last seen it — a line of six naked men, their backs covered with welts, looking over their shoulders to see why the door has just opened. Beside them stands a young trainee in a blue uniform, a long whip in his right hand, looking surprised and terrified as he glances first at us and then at the beefy trainer at his side.

No one says a word. Dr. Mirsch gives a startled little whimper, which seems to hang over the silent tableau like a flag. This scene of frozen horror is almost funny, but the humor is crushed beneath a jumble of memories that fall on me like bricks from a collapsing wall.

"Come on, let's go," I say to Dr. Mirsch, my voice suddenly tired and empty.

I close the door gently, as if apologizing for interrupting a high-level committee meeting. Dr. Mirsch follows closely behind me, and when I glance back, I see that his head is slumped forward and down, as if he has just plunged into a terrible depression.

We pass through the tunnel silently and take the elevator back to the lobby. I sign out, and the guard makes some inane comment about the weather. All of this happens as if in a dream, because both of us are still stuck in the room below, our faces frozen in disbelief and horror at a scene that even I had come to believe could never happen.

"What does this mean?" Dr. Mirsch asks on the way to the car.

"It means what I told you it means, Dr. Mirsch," I say in a voice more gentle than before. "It means they are training people to be more productive, to be more effective, to be able to suffer any indignity, impose any pain, in order to win out against the competition."

Dr. Mirsch does not answer. We ride back to his office in silence. I do not lie down on the couch, but sit across the room from him in the other easy chair.

Dr. Mirsch doesn't touch the bag of cookies on the stand beside him. He sits staring at me, stroking his mustache, his eyes watery.

"Look," I begin, "I'm sorry. I shouldn't have grabbed you like that, kidnaped you and forced you to go see that. But it was the only way I could prove it to you — and to myself."

"Why did you need me?"

"Well, two pairs of eyes are better than one. Or, put another way, an ounce of reality is worth a pound of cure."

"What do you want to do now?" he asks.

"I don't know. What do you want to do? You're the doctor."

"Let's think it over. I've got to have time to absorb this. This is, of course, unique in my experience. With your permission, I would like to consult one or two of my colleagues. The implications of all this reach much further than your own progress in treatment. There are ethical and moral dimensions that must be considered. There are economic aspects, too, that must be taken into account. All in all, we need time to think."

I don't like Mirsch's reference to "economic aspects," but I do agree that we need time to absorb and reflect. For one thing, I have to decide whether I want to proceed alone in the very possible event that he decides to withdraw.

"Okay, fine with me. When do you want to see me?"

"Let's make it day after tomorrow. Four o'clock sound all right?"

"Sure."

32

IT IS MONDAY MORNING, and I am back in my office with its pornographic luxury and stifling silence. Why would anyone want this kind of life? What this office really amounts to is a top-of-the-line casket, a splendid bronze sarcophagus lined with satin and attended by a dozen fawning morticians, so obliging and artificial that you would like to beat them back into humanity. The office is a terrible disappointment, I conclude, but not the kind of disappointment that I could easily give up.

What to do? If I depend on Dr. Mirsch's advice, I don't have to make any decision myself. But I might find his advice unacceptable. For instance, suppose he suggests I forget about the whole thing? Or suppose he wants us to call a massive press conference of some sort to reveal the whole sordid scandal? Well, in the first instance, if I forget the whole thing, can I really bring myself to live with the memories of Room 111? And, in the second scenario, what would be the aftermath of the massive press conference? Probably very little of it would ever appear in the newspapers or on television —

far too dangerous stuff for that. And besides, the general reaction among the media people who attend the press conference might tend to be on the Company side, an attempt at understanding, something like: "But we have to compete with the Japanese, don't we? After all, the Japanese have executive training programs."

I had seen the scenes on television myself — young Japanese executives undergoing nightmarish training at some Spartan camp in the mountains. Standing rigidly while some bulky samurai screams abuse at them. Rising in a group to confess, amid sobs, their awful incompetence. Walking to the center of a crowded railroad station and singing their company song at the top of their voices, the better to prove their loyalty and courage.

Well, they were doing all that, so why should I find the Company's executive training program so offensive? It was only a short step, after all, from accepting the abuse of a corporate drill sergeant in Japan to submitting to the more sophisticated rigors of the Trainorium, with its elaborate postmedieval torture machines.

I pull myself back. This kind of thinking can only confuse me, delay a decision. I must concentrate on the binary issue: to accept or reject. To accept the $300,000 salary, the $250,000 bonus, the limousine, the fawning subordinates, the unlimited expense account, the power and recognition. Or to reject it in favor of truth, integrity, sanity, decency — whatever those things are. Whose battle was I fighting, anyway?

This afternoon I will see Dr. Mirsch again. Maybe he will offer a middle course. Maybe he will propose an ingenious compromise. Maybe he will deny that he saw anything extraordinary on Saturday. Maybe he will come up with a way out for both of us.

But as things turn out, Dr. Mirsch doesn't get a chance to say anything about the matter. Only an hour or so before I am to leave the office for my appointment, Kreiznach comes barging in, smiling broadly and full of excitement. He closes the door behind him, pulls a chair right up to my desk, and announces the reason for his surprise visit.

"You've got a new assignment," he begins, "an assignment that is certainly the most important of your career — so far, anyway."

I have never seen him more excited.

"Okay. Let's have it. But first try to calm down."

"Well, the Chairman has asked you to take charge of the most important press conference in the history of the Company. Since it's only two weeks away and will be attended by two to three hundred of the country's top media people, you are really going to have to scramble."

"And may I ask what this press conference is all about?"

Kreiznach smiles and reaches for his briefcase.

"Here is an outline of the whole thing. Since it runs twelve pages, single spaced, I won't wait for you to read it. But I will give you a brief rundown.

"This press conference is being held to announce that we are starting a new executive training program called Exec-Excel. Originally, we were going to announce this in the land surveyors speech. Remember, the Chairman said he would have an important announcement? Well, he decided it was much too important for that occasion, which explains this press conference.

"Now, Exec-Excel may not knock you out of your chair, but this is no ordinary training program. What makes it so important is that it is such a great leap forward in the history of managerial development — the greatest ever made. This program has been in the planning stage for five years, and its development has cost us somewhere in the neighborhood of twelve million dollars. The work that has gone into it is unbelievable — a task force of a hundred and fifty people working full time. We've had the best thinking of psychologists, personnel people, physicians, sociologists, health experts, criminologists — you name it — the task force included representatives of every discipline dealing with human behavior."

"Criminologists?"

"Yes. That may seem a bit far out, but we've taken a long, hard look at the effects of various kinds of punishment on human behavior. And of course we've taken an equally close look at the effects of reward on human behavior.

"The exciting thing, though, is that this is not just our effort. It's a joint program developed by our team and the Japanese. As you may know, the Japanese are way ahead of us in this kind of thing. So shortly after we got going on our program, we sent a team to Japan to study the situation there. The Japanese were doing amazing things. They were far ahead of us, but we pulled out all the stops, and with their help — for which they were well paid, incidentally — we have now caught up.

"So anyway, all the people involved in this, from the Chairman on down, are terribly excited about it, because we're going to be telling the world about the most revolutionary development in managerial training in history. And you're going to be in charge."

Although I can see that the whole program might be interesting, I fail to share Kreiznach's excitement.

"Uh, well, when will it be held?"

"Two weeks from tomorrow, starting at ten A.M. and lasting till four."

"Why so long?"

"We have a lot to tell and show."

"Where is it going to be held?"

"Room 111."

"Room 111? You must be kidding! Are you crazy? What if they see the machines?"

Kreiznach looks at me incredulously.

"You don't seem to understand. The machines are an important part of the program. In fact, the entire training program in the Troubled Employee Department — of which you are one of our most distinguished graduates — the entire training program has been serving as a kind of testing ground for the procedures that have now been incorporated into Exec-Excel."

"Procedures."

"Yes, procedures."

"You mean like torture, sadism, whipping — that sort of thing?"

Kreiznach smiles indulgently. "Those are just words. You know the proper words for these programs. Management Adaptability Seminar is a good example."

"Well, I don't know."

"Look, we're counting on you. The Chairman is counting on you. You're a natural because of your skills and experience, but also because you're a graduate of the program itself. At least you are a graduate of a program that closely resembles what Exec-Excel will be in its final form."

"And you're going to show all of this to the media, as if it is something to be proud of?"

"Why, of course. It *is* something to be proud of. Look, we've got some material written already that describes the rationale for all of this. We've got a flood of statistics that show its proven worth. This is the most carefully researched, the most thoroughly tested, program of its kind in the history of human management. It's something we are very, very proud of, and it's something you will also be proud of, once you've had a chance to study the material, look at some of our videotapes from Japan, and see how great this thing is."

Kreiznach pulls a huge pile of documents and photographs from his briefcase and drops them on my desk. He gets up, returns the chair to its proper place, and comes back to my desk with outstretched hand.

"Congratulations! I know the Chairman will be pleased with your enthusiasm. I look forward to working with you on this. We'll have almost unlimited resources — a budget of a million dollars and a conference staff of a hundred. The first meeting of the executive committee is at ten A.M. tomorrow. I'll see you there. Incidentally, all of this is very secret. Two weeks from tomorrow, when we drop this bombshell, it is going to explode as the most important business story of the decade!"

Kreiznach's abrupt departure on the heels of his stunning announcement leaves me in a state of semishock. The whole idea is preposterous, and I am about to call him back to tell him I am refusing the assignment when my buzzer sounds.

"It's Mr. Kreiznach, sir."

"Listen," he says, his voice still high with excitement, "I forgot one of the most important things. If the Chairman judges this press conference a success, it means a bonus of one million dollars for you. That ought to help you make up your mind!"

This latest piece of news is hardly less spectacular than what he told me only a few minutes before. A million dollars? That's unbelievable. It doesn't change the basic nature of the problem — whether I should lend my talent and my name to the promotion of something as insane as Exec-Excel. But the million-dollar bonus does give me a new, once-in-a-lifetime opportunity. Take the money and run. Leave this insane corporate world once and for all. Because if I don't get the money, someone else will, and I'll be stuck here for the rest of my life.

I pick up the phone and dial Dr. Mirsch's number. I tell him what has happened, but I don't tell him that I have had any doubts about accepting the assignment. Instead, I talk enthusiastically about what it will mean to my career, how important the whole program will be to the country's industrial renaissance. By the time I finish, I find myself believing everything I have told him. The phone call spells the end of my dilemma over the whole experience in Room 111 and its aftermath. No longer will I debate the question of silence versus public disclosure. I have opted for public disclosure, only the circumstances and outcome will be far different, and far better for me, than I had ever imagined.

33

THE TROUBLED EMPLOYEE DEPARTMENT, now called simply Exec-Excel, has been completely refurbished in preparation for today's "historic" event. Everything has been painted; gone is the institutional green I had hated on first sight. In its place is a Wedgwood effect, deep blue with white trim, new carpeting throughout, new furniture, and a new auditorium built with no thought of expense. Altogether, a very pleasant complex of training rooms and living quarters whose existence in the basement of the building, lavishly outfitted with the latest electronic devices and an astounding array of "athletic" equipment, will surely impress even the most blasé reporter.

The auditorium is full, and I take my place on the stage with an assortment of dignitaries from the Company and our Japanese collaborators. Only moments ago, Kreiznach triumphantly informed me that only two of the three hundred invitees failed to show up. The clock shows nine fifty-five, which means only five minutes until the Chairman makes his entrance. Why am I so nervous? All of this has been rehearsed ad nauseam. Every detail has been gone over time and again, from the design and accuracy of the name badges to the quality of the lettuce in the shrimp cocktail. The Chairman has driven us mad for the last two weeks with his continuous barrage of questions, his constant criticism and carping. But now he seems pleased, and at yesterday's final rehearsal he gave me a big pat on the back and his best smile.

"Flawless. Absolutely perfect," he said. "Now just do it again in the morning."

And do it we will. The clock points to ten exactly now, and from the wing to my left I can see the Chairman's ample form, followed by two vice presidents, make its way onto the stage and up to the podium.

Right on cue, applause breaks out throughout the auditorium, an outburst prompted by a couple of dozen of our own people scattered through the room. The media people join in reluctantly, and the Chairman smiles his million-dollar smile.

The Chairman is at his very best. Reading from a concealed TelePrompTer, his gestures rehearsed to perfection, he conveys an inspired blend of confidence, exuberance, good will, intelligence, and camaraderie.

"Never before," he says, "have so many distinguished representatives of the media gathered together for a company press conference, and never before have they had such good reason to do so. Nobody in this room will be disappointed by what they see and hear today, because this is one of the most important developments in the history of American business.

"Not since the industrial revolution," the Chairman says, "has the world of business witnessed a development of this magnitude. Even the advent of the computer age pales by comparison with the managerial revolution, in which the true potential of leadership will be exploited for the first time in history. The power of computers — indeed, the power of the atom — is nothing compared to the explosive power of human beings stretched to the very limit of their capacity. Here, in this building, we now have the capacity to create Fords, Eatons, Carnegies, Mellons, Kaisers, by the hundreds, men and women of almost unimaginable vision, whose ability to inspire and direct underlings has been matched by only a very few people in the entire history of industrial society."

The Chairman goes on for ten minutes in this vein, and when he finishes and sits down, accompanied by rather tepid applause, the room fills with martial music.

A line of Japanese, wearing identical dark blue suits and striped ties, marches onto the stage and begins executing a series of intricate maneuvers — forward to the center of the stage, then branching off to each side, turning abruptly to march to the rear, joining precisely and resuming their parade in double ranks, crossing through each other's lines, shifting abruptly to slow step, then to double time — all with the precision of machines. Meanwhile, in the background, a deep voice explains what is going on.

"Ladies and gentlemen, the Japanese Executive Drill Team! This group of men, more than any other body in Japan, illustrates the superb discipline and dedication of your average Japanese executive. When we talk of teamwork in the United States, it means one thing. But in Japan teamwork has an entirely different meaning — a group of people who are willing to give their lives for their company's cause, a group of people who will work endless hours under the most difficult conditions to achieve the goals their company has set for them. This is what the Japanese mean by teamwork! Watch them now as they go through their paces!"

Abruptly, the Japanese drill team stops in a line across the stage. Suddenly, their arms and legs moving like robots, they quickly remove their suits and fling them to the back of the stage, dressing ranks and snapping to attention in blue and white tank tops and shorts.

"Now, ladies and gentlemen, watch closely while the Japanese Executive Drill Team performs the Forward Planning Committee Ballet," the loudspeaker voice intones.

The small, muscular bodies of the drill team glide gracefully across the stage to the sounds of the waltz from *Tales of Hoffmann*. Their coordination is perfect, and as their bodies twist and gyrate in exquisite variation, the unmistakable corporate half smile can be seen in perfect form on every face. Their movement is stately and dignified, yet forceful and full of purpose; no matter how slight the motions, they are carried out in perfect unison, the total effect being that of a single dancer on the stage.

"Ladies and gentlemen, there you have an example of teamwork! And let me remind you, these young executives have perfected this performance through countless hours of practice after and *before* reporting for work. That's right, before. Many of their practice sessions began at four in the morning! So let's hear it for the Japanese Executive Drill Team!"

To my surprise, the announcer's words bring a loud burst of applause from the audience, which up to now has not been very responsive to any of the activities on the stage.

"Thank you, thank you," the announcer says. "And now, for a change of pace, let's take a look at an entirely different aspect of executive training as practiced in Japan and as soon to be practiced here through our Exec-Excel program. I'm speaking of subordination, the capacity to put the welfare of the group above the welfare of the individual. An old-fashioned word for this might be humility, but for right now we're calling it subordination — executive subordination, if you will. Watch, now, as our Japanese colleagues demonstrate how abuse can strengthen the will and persuade even the most egocentric person to abandon childish ways and work for the benefit of the group."

The curtain opens again, revealing two Japanese men in identical business suits. One of them is enormous, probably six feet five and at least two hundred and fifty pounds. The other is very small, almost a midget, and has a fierce expression on his face. The smaller man is pacing back and forth in what appears to be a very genuine rage. He begins shouting at the giant, who stands at attention, looking at his feet in a posture of abject humility.

"You lowly worm. You unprecedented fool. If a pigeon had your brains he would fly backward. You are not worthy to work for this company. You are the essence of incompetence. You are so incredibly dumb that even your mother would throw you out. What are you? How do you perceive yourself?"

Staring straight down, the giant replies in a toneless voice: "I am only a worm. I am the lowest of worms."

"Go on!" the midget screams.

"I am unworthy to work for this company. In every aspect, I am far below the required standards."

"Tell everyone about your latest mistake, your latest example of incompetence!"

The giant begins sobbing loudly, building to a crescendo that reaches to the last rows of the auditorium.

"I overestimated our quarterly sales by twelve percent."

"And how did this happen, worst of fools?"

"Through inattention to details, through sloth and ignorance, through inadequate dedication to my company and my coworkers," the giant says, sobbing.

"And how will you atone for this stupid error? How will you try to make yourself worthy of your company's confidence?"

Sobbing as loudly as ever, the giant bends forward in a deep bow and speaks in a voice of genuine contrition:

"By perfect adherence to the founder's principles, which are: unwavering loyalty, total dedication, complete humility, and subservience to the will of my colleagues."

"Very well, worm. That's good for now. But your behavior will be monitored closely during the next month. Remember, if your performance is anything less than outstanding, you will be made to describe your incompetence and unworthiness — shout it at the top of your voice — in the center of the company cafeteria. Do you understand?"

"Oh, yes, yes, I understand," the giant says in a broken voice. "Just give me this chance — one more chance — and I promise you will not be disappointed in me."

With this, the two turn toward the audience and bow deeply, but the giant continues sobbing even as he leaves the stage. It is clear to everyone in the room that the giant has not been acting. As if to confirm this, the voice of the announcer blasts out:

"And there you have it, a display of genuine atonement and contrition on the part of the larger man. The participants in this scene were not actors, but real people employed in a large Nagasaki factory. And the incident described — the erroneous sales estimate — actually happened. Our guests from the American media can see from this demonstration, I'm sure, the level of discipline that exists in Japan and why that country's productivity growth has so consistently outdistanced ours."

The Chairman mounts the podium again to announce the next event on the schedule. He reads from his invisible Tele-PrompTer but interrupts himself in a nicely handled ad lib:

"Look, I just want to say at this point that I hope none of you has the idea that Exec-Excel is just a carbon copy of Japanese techniques. While we have been influenced by the Japanese, we've given our program a distinctly American flavor, as you will see as you get further into the day's activities.

"And now, for what I'm sure many of you will remember as the highlight of this historic event, you will be escorted to our Trainorium to see the latest endurance machines — all American designed and built. And while it was not judged practical to let you experience these machines fully, we decided to give each of you the opportunity to sit in them — or lie on them — just to get the feel of what our trainees will experience."

The Trainorium is hardly recognizable from the horrible days when it held me in its painful grip. It is freshly painted, with a new, brighter tile floor and the walls lined with plush furniture, magazine racks, and potted plants. Altogether, it gives the impression of an athletic club, except for the balloons hanging from the ceiling, the red, white, and blue bunting that emphasizes the American cast to the program, and the pretty models at the machines who explain their workings to the media people who crowd around.

I walk over to Machine Number 1 to watch a model describe it.

"Actually," she is saying, "this particular machine is one of the favorites among our trainees. They like it because it is one of the most rigorous machines on the floor. Its purpose is to show the trainee that he can stretch himself farther than he ever imagined. Mastering this machine means he will be able to stretch himself to the maximum in his job."

"Is this machine painful?" a bearded television reporter shouts from the edge of the group.

"Yes, of course," the model answers, smiling smoothly. "All of these machines are painful, because that is the only way we can teach our trainees endurance and the only way we can test their capacity for difficult challenges. But I want to emphasize that none of these machines is in the least harmful. The condition of the trainee is continuously monitored by a variety of sensors on the machine. We know at any point his blood pressure, pulse, temperature, and various other factors. There is no danger at all."

"Has anyone ever been injured on these machines?" another reporter asks.

"Absolutely not," the attendant replies. "These have all been tested to the limit, and there is no way — let me repeat, no way — that a trainee can be permanently harmed."

This is a little too much for me to take, and I turn to leave as one of the reporters stretches out on the machine, smiling over his shoulder at his colleagues.

I walk around the packed Trainorium, pushing my way through the people. The machines are very popular with the media people, and long lines begin to form at each of them as the reporters clamber to try them out. The room is beginning to get a little warm, thanks to the throng and the television lights that seem to be everywhere.

I am a little surprised at the mood — festive and enthusiastic. Reporters shout at each other to try out the various machines, flirt with the models, and press around one of the three well-stocked bars.

After lunch, the happy group returns to the auditorium for the final events, the last of which will be a question-and-answer period. For a while we were very worried about this part, but the Chairman has spent days studying briefing books and subjecting himself to mock sessions in which we take the part of reporters. The result of all this preparation is that every one of us, from the Chairman on down, is confident that he can handle anything the reporters throw at him.

I leave my place on the stage to watch the proceedings from the last row of the auditorium. The reporters are not paying much attention to what's happening on the stage. They are talking loudly to one another, cracking jokes and comparing notes.

"What are you gonna write?" a reporter sitting in the row in front of me asks the man next to him.

"Oh, I'm going to say it's a good program. It's about time this country did something like this. The Japs have gotten way ahead of us. We can't just sit around letting them increase their lead."

"Yeah," answers his colleague. "I think it's a historic step forward. That may sound a bit corny, but I really believe that. I've talked to the office a couple of times, and my editors want me to pull out all the stops. We've got a new emphasis on business news, you know, and I guess they're going to spread this across the top of page one."

Onstage, the Japanese-American Executive Drill Team is winding up its act. This is the final event before the question-and-answer period, and it was designed to be a spectacular demonstration of U.S.-Japanese cooperation. The flags of the two countries wave in the breeze created by offstage fans, and the auditorium is filled with martial and patriotic music from both countries. The hundred-member team, made up of the best young executives from the Company and the Japanese delegation, struts through the complex drill with astounding precision. As they march offstage, the audience erupts in loud applause that lasts a full two minutes, the longest I have ever heard from any audience of media people.

A beaming Chairman takes his place at the podium, gestures for silence, and asks for questions. The reporters are eager, and the questions fly out in rapid succession. They are answered smoothly and quickly by the confident Chairman, who is glowing in the success of the day and the challenge of the moment.

"Do you really believe, sir, that this kind of program can raise U.S. productivity?"

"Of course I do. If I didn't think so, we wouldn't be starting it. Study after study shows us that we are on the right course. Let me tell you, too, that many other companies are planning to follow our lead as soon as we show the way."

"Sir, isn't there kind of a sadistic quality to some of this program — like the machines in the Trainorium, for instance?"

"We don't see it as sadistic at all. I guess you might say that one man's sadism is another man's challenge. We are determined to develop a new breed of executive, far more disciplined, far more dedicated to his company, than those of this or previous generations. Sure, the training can be tough, but we have been more than gratified by the response of our graduates. Most of them come to us and thank us for what they've gone through, saying it was the most valuable experience of their lives, that it has completely reshaped their attitude toward their work and their colleagues."

The Chairman fields every question flawlessly, and when he finishes, the media people break out in another loud round of applause, during which the Chairman leaves the stage, smiling and waving to the crowd, his face glowing with triumph.

In the corridor, Kreiznach rushes up to me and shakes my hand enthusiastically.

"You did it! You did it!" he says, almost weeping with gratitude. "That was a million-dollar job if ever there was one."

Kreiznach tells me the Chairman wants to see me in his office as soon as I can get there. I take the executive elevator to the thirty-second floor and brush past the smiling guards, who now greet me with an especially pleasant "Good afternoon, sir."

The Chairman is ecstatic, shakes my hand repeatedly, offers me a drink, tells me that my career is secure and that I am obviously on the ladder to the top.

"I have never seen anything handled so well before in my career." The Chairman beams. "Let me tell you, you've come a long way since that flight we made together to Los Angeles — a long way, indeed. It's as if you are a different man, a complete transformation, and all for the better. Let me thank you again and tell you that you did a splendid job — just splendid."

With this, the Chairman walks over to his desk, takes something from a drawer, and walks back, handing me an envelope.

"Well, open it up," the Chairman says. "I had it prepared in advance, just in case." There are tears in the Chairman's eyes.

I open the envelope and remove a check, made out to me for a million dollars.

Once more, the Chairman grasps my hand and shakes it vigorously.

I, too, am overcome.

"Thank you, sir," I mumble. "It's been an honor and a pleasure to serve you on such an important project, and I am glad you are so pleased with the outcome."

With that, I leave his office, feeling somewhat foolish as I head down the corridor, still grasping the million-dollar check.

34

I AM SUMMONED to a meeting with Marlott, Stelritz, and Kreiznach. There is no hint of what it's about, but as soon as I take my seat in the small conference room, I realize it's about me.

"Sit down, sit down," says Kreiznach in his best echospeak form. "We've been looking forward to talking to you since you completed your training. Well, actually, you didn't complete your training, but I'll get into that in a minute.

"Yes, all three of us have wanted this chance, looked forward to this opportunity, to meet with you and exchange a few ideas about your current situation and where you go from here."

Kreiznach pauses to gaze out the window and collect his thoughts. Please, please get to the point, Charlie. And Marlott. God, I wish he would just vanish — sitting opposite me looking particularly sullen, glaring, in fact, so angry is he at my new prominence. Stelritz? Stelritz is just Stelritz, Mr. Efficiency, half smiling down at a pad on which he is busily scribbling notes. About what? About the civilities Kreiznach has just unloaded on me? What a collection of fools.

"Anyway," Kreiznach resumes, "you may not have known this, but the three of us constitute your training committee. Have all along, watched you like a proud father teaching his son to swim and seeing the boy gradually get the hang of it. Well, you got the hang of it, certainly, and generally the three of us and the others in charge of your case in the department are very pleased with your progress."

"Most of the others," Marlott interrupts.

"Yes, most of the others," Kreiznach says, slightly annoyed. "Anyway, there's just one thing hanging fire. And that is that you never really completed the program. Oh, I'm not talking about your hurried defection. That was quite understandable, even though it was the first time it had ever happened. The point is that you were very distraught, and maybe you thought the idea of giving a little discipline to some strangers was something you couldn't accept.

"Anyway, that's not really what I had in mind. What I'm getting at is this. Even if you had stuck it out through that, ah, disciplinary session with the whips and all, even if you had seen that through to the finish, you would have had one more hurdle to jump."

"Kind of a high hurdle," Stelritz mutters without looking up.

Kreiznach laughs excessively. Marlott just sits there gazing at me belligerently.

"Well, yes, a high hurdle, depending on your point of view. The fact is that it is a rather tough thing to do, for most people, and we in Administration can understand that. Tough, but necessary, because it is the perfect test of your loyalty to the Company."

Silence. A long silence.

"A test of my loyalty?" I ask.

"Well, yes, perhaps not so much a test as an affirmation. An affirmation because we already believe in your loyalty to the Company. This is by way of confirming it."

"Yes, confirmation," Stelritz says with a deep chuckle.

There is another long silence. It is obvious that Kreiznach is having a lot of trouble getting to the point. This does not encourage me.

"You see," he continues, "the time may come in the course of your career here when you are asked to perform some particularly onerous duty. We would assume, of course, that you would carry out your orders without question. Most people would, and the three of us are firmly of the opinion that you would be among that group.

"Still, what we think is beside the point. There are procedures to follow, and just because you are a friend of ours, we can't make an exception."

"No exceptions," Marlott interjects, a pleased look on his face.

"So to the task at hand, the question of the test, the final vow of loyalty. In your case, it will involve your good friend Conrad. We want you to take appropriate action against him."

"You mean you want me to fire him?"

"Not exactly."

"Exactly what, then?"

"We want you to deal with him with extreme prejudice."

"You've got to be kidding. You mean you want me to kill him?"

Nobody answers. Silence fills the room like a bad smell, and you can almost hear the tension.

"Look," Stelritz says, staring straight at me with his best kamikaze smile, "Conrad is of no use to you or to anybody in the Company. Ordinarily, we would fire him in an instant — a more orthodox final solution to the Conrad question than the one we're proposing. But orthodoxy is not what we're after. We need proof, positive proof of your total loyalty to the Company."

I think of the SS men who trained their beautiful German shepherds for months and then were asked to shoot them in the same kind of loyalty test.

"I don't think I can do that," I say after a long interval.

"Think about it," Marlott says. "Give it some thought. After all, it's just your whole career."

Kreiznach nods vigorously. "He put it well, I'm afraid. It is your whole career, and while you may balk at the idea at this point, that's understandable. When you've had a chance to think about it for a while, you will see, I believe, that it's a reasonable test for a man who someday will be in control of millions of dollars in company funds and thousands of jobs."

"Will be in control?" I ask.

"I'm convinced of it. All of the auguries are there. You've got an unbelievably bright future here, and you could very easily go right to the top. But we want you to take on this final burden. It will be difficult, we concede that, but it will be over quickly. And then you will be, well, you'll be cleared for your destiny, if I may say so."

I know that I won't do this thing they are asking of me. But I find myself acting as if I might.

"How am I supposed to accomplish this mission?"

"With this," Kreiznach says, reaching into his briefcase and pulling out a pistol.

I take it in my hand. It is a Walther, considerably shopworn, of the type used by the Gestapo. Where in hell did Kreiznach put his hands on it? I am afraid to ask.

I slip the pistol into my coat pocket. I feel as if I am acting in some third-rate movie. I smile a large, phony smile, a smile of superb confidence and insouciance.

"Well, let me think it over. How long do I have?"

"We need your answer by tomorrow," Kreiznach replies. "Take the rest of the day off. Go home. Go to the park. Go to a movie. Relax. Use the time to give it your best thought. And then get back to us first thing in the morning. I'm sure when you've had a chance to review all the pros and cons, you'll see that there is only one answer you can give us. And you know what that is."

"Okay, gentlemen, I guess that's it," Kreiznach says.

Stelritz grabs his notepad and rushes out the door. Kreiznach reaches over and shakes my hand. Marlott walks over to the window and stares at the sky. I can hardly get out of the room fast enough.

35

IN THE EVENT, Conrad's death was not a great problem. Although he was sullen to the end, I had the impression he went willingly enough. Maybe he was ready to sacrifice his life to save my career. I'll never know. What I do know is that the episode turned out to be much less painful than I had anticipated. In fact, it was hardly painful at all.

"How are things going?" I asked him on the walk to his car. He always parked at the farthest limit of the lot, as if to prolong the time it took to get to the office. Now the lot was practically deserted, dimly lit in the Company's new drive to save energy, and money along with it.

He didn't answer me immediately but trudged along with his head down. Maybe he was mad at me for walking out to his car with him. I told him I wanted to talk to him about a speech, and that I needed the exercise.

"They're going just like they always go," he said finally. "Bad. Abominably bad. The pits. The fourth ring of hell."

"Yes, well, maybe things will get better. I hear there's a reorganization brewing."

"Again? Yet another reorganization. It's only a dance of villains, the thugs' tarantella, the goons' gavotte. What does it mean to me? To you, maybe it will be something wonderful. You're on a steady course up. But to me it means only that different people come around to slip food into my cell and open the door to let me out for the exercise period."

Conrad's bitterness was terminal, which made my job a lot easier. After all, he had outlived his usefulness to the Company — if, indeed, he had ever had any. They say that at one time, years ago, he was a pretty good speechwriter. But now he was burned out. He would sit in front of the typewriter for an hour or so, staring at a blank piece of paper and uttering solemn curses.

Oh, I still had some affection for him. He could be very funny, and I used to think his comments on what went on around us were hilarious. But lately I had begun to take a different view. I saw him now as a negative influence on those around him, a man who spread calumny about the Company while accepting its generous pay and benefits.

No, Conrad's time had come. When we reached his car, in the last row of spaces in the lot, we stopped while he fumbled for his key in the darkness. There was no moon, and the nearest light was several hundred feet away. I took him by the arm.

"Conrad, old buddy, you know that this is the end of the road for you," I said.

"What do you mean?" His face looked old and drawn, his skin gray in the pallid light.

"I mean that I'm going to kill you."

"Why?" He did not seem especially alarmed.

"Company orders."

"Oh." He looked into the dark woods that began a few

yards away. "I guess there's no way out? No, there wouldn't be. Company orders. I know they mean a lot to you."

For an instant his passivity frightened me. I had expected him to resist strongly, hit me, run, shout, scream. But then, after I had time to think about it, I realized that he had no hitting, no running, no shouting, no screaming, left in him.

Just as I was about to reach for the pistol, he raised his hand in a plea to delay.

"No," I said, "we have to get it over with."

"I've got to know," he murmured. "I've got to know about the sightings. The dog, the pigeons, Blanders and Stein, the screaming woman. Were they real? Did those things really happen? Or were they arranged?"

I admired Conrad's curiosity, one of his most endearing qualities. But it was hardly the time to answer. Anyway, I didn't have an answer.

"I don't know," I said. "I just don't know. Yes, Blanders and Stein exist. I saw them just a couple of days ago. I suspect they had been off for a while in the Troubled Employee Department. Somebody goofed, went around and removed their buttons from all the intercoms.

"As for the other things, your guess is as good as mine. I know the Chairman keeps pigeons. Maybe the guards were training them or something. On the other hand, it seems to me I may have dreamed that about the Chairman's pigeons.

"The screaming woman? I assume she had escaped from the Troubled Employee Department. She may have been a trainee, or she may have been a very troubled trainer. Again, it's something we'll never know."

"What does it all mean?" Conrad asked. "Why couldn't we ever find out why things happened, who was behind everything? Everything was a secret, it was all a mystery."

"Yes, the Company is a mystery. Maybe we have no need to know. Maybe the mystery keeps it going, keeps fear up, pumps up ambition, keeps things churning, provides the whole thing with power and drive."

"You know what I say?" Conrad asked, putting his hand on my shoulder.

"No, Jim, what do you say?"

"I say doodah. That's what it's all about — doodah."

Those were Conrad's last words. I pulled the Walther quickly from my coat pocket and pressed it against his chest. He looked down at the gun and fell back against the car with a faint whimper.

He was smiling when I pulled the trigger. The report was quieter than I had expected. He slumped sideways, then slowly to the pavement, his head resting against a hubcap. I thought it was somehow fitting that he should end his life so close to one of the Company's products. He had always loved cars; next to dying in an auto accident, this was the best thing for him.

I returned the gun to my pocket and headed back to the building at a brisk walk. I knew there would be no trouble because certain arrangements had been made. Key people in Security had been alerted to keep their people away from that end of the parking lot and to ignore any loud sounds they might hear. When Conrad's body was found, probably the next morning, his wallet and wristwatch would be missing. It was one of those horrible things that happen these days, a stickup in a dark parking lot. There had been a few incidents during the past year, but this was the first time anyone had ever been murdered. Unfortunately, the police would find no clues. It might have been one of the tough youngsters who were seen increasingly in the area. They were hard to identify, it was said. But, in any event, no one would report seeing anybody.

Conrad's funeral was surprisingly well attended. I was asked to give the eulogy. I praised his great talent, his devotion to the Company, his charm, and his surpassing wit. It was a terrible tragedy, I said, that a man of such promise could lose his life in such a senseless and untimely way. His friends, his colleagues in the Company, and the Company itself would feel a gap. I looked up once or twice during my speech and could see Conrad's widow, a red-haired woman with thin lips and thick glasses, sitting in the front row beside her long-haired son. They looked at me strangely, I thought, not with a look of bereavement so much as with a look of hatred. But I suppose this was only my imagination. There was no reason at all for them to doubt that Conrad had met his death exactly as the authorities had reported.

On the way out of the church, Kreiznach came down the steps close behind me. As he passed by, he gave me a faint smile and spoke softly out of the corner of his mouth:

"You passed, with flying colors. Well done. You're on your way!"

When I reached the sidewalk, Stelritz approached. He looked happy, extremely happy. Waving his arm at the long line of limousines in front of the church, he beamed.

"You know," he said, "I think old Conrad would have been very pleased with this. Look at them, twenty-five of our Brougham de Villes, all just off the assembly line, all the same Aegean blue. What a sight! It's a real company funeral for Conrad. And he thought we never liked him."

36

THE RETURNS from the press conference are phenomenal —
hundreds and hundreds of newspaper and magazine clippings
and hundreds of videotapes from all the major networks and
stations across the country. Underlying all this publicity is a
strong current of approval.

"One American company is finally doing something about
meeting the challenge of the Japanese" is a typical opening
on a television report; COMPANY INVENTS DISCIPLINE TO MEET
JAPANESE THREAT, a typical headline. The editorials speak
glowingly of "industrial statesmanship," "new economic order," "the return of the work ethic," and a "massive breakthrough in American management."

Even though the press conference was not my idea, I find
myself reaping most of the credit for it. Taking advantage of
the situation, I send out a continuous flow of reports on the
reaction to it, assembling an assortment of stories into a book

entitled *Room 111: The Company Meets the Press.* I distribute this book to more than a hundred of the top executives. They, in turn, react with highly laudatory memos that I assemble into another book for distribution to a handful of executives at the top.

The result of all this is that I become something of an overnight legend in the Company. I begin worrying about my new prominence and decide I must begin to take steps to lower my profile. So even though I conscientiously attend the meetings of all the committees I serve on, I try not to say much, smoking my pipe and nodding in agreement on the rare occasions when I decide to speak.

I find that I am treated with the utmost deference wherever I go, by the waitresses in the vice-presidential dining room, by the guards at the various stations around the building, by my colleagues, subordinates, and even my few superiors.

I decide to have my office refurbished in a colonial American motif. When it is all finished, I find myself spending a surprising amount of time just sitting at my desk admiring the surroundings or enjoying the view through the broad expanse of windows that cover two sides of my corner office. I did receive a little static from the Accounting Department about the cost of the remodeling job, but they were very polite and emphasized that they only wanted a little more information for their records.

Every once in a while I encounter one of my old colleagues from the dinners in Room 111. In fact, three of them serve with me on the Forward Planning Committee — hearty fellows who never fail to give me some interesting inside gossip from the sports world. One day I had occasion to see a videotape of one of this committee's meetings. I can't remember why I was watching it — apparently because I needed to know something about the discussion we had held. But anyway, there I was, cleaning my pipe during a long-winded, particularly boring presentation by some flunky from the Finance Department. To tell the truth, I had a little trouble recognizing myself at first. I looked a lot younger than I thought I did, convincing evidence that the long hours I've been spending in the vice-presidential exercise room are paying handsome dividends.

One day about a month after the press conference, my secretary buzzes.

"Mr. Turner is here for his ten o'clock appointment, sir."

"Who?"

"Mr. Turner, the young man from Media Relations who is up for the Exec-Excel program."

"Oh, I remember now. Send him in."

Turner is the kind of young executive whose career stops dead in the water in his early thirties, for reasons understood by everyone except himself. I understand the reasons perfectly as Turner sits down in front of me, fidgeting, smiling awkwardly, clearing his throat, and doing everything he can think of to create the image of what we've begun to call the anti-executive.

"How do you feel about going into Exec-Excel?" I ask this self-conscious young man.

"Oh, fine, fine, I guess," Turner says.

"You guess. That's kind of an odd response."

"What do you mean, sir?"

"Well, if you don't know, maybe you shouldn't have been chosen. It is something of an honor, you know."

"Oh, I'm sure it is. Er, I guess I shouldn't have said 'I guess.' I mean, I just shouldn't have said it."

"Well, you will benefit from the program immensely. Are you in any way apprehensive?"

"Well, to tell the truth, I am a bit. You hear a lot of stories."

"There is no cause to worry, none at all," I assure him, lighting my pipe and blowing the smoke upward in huge, billowing puffs. It strikes me right then that this gesture alone is a distinct sign that I am very much in command of the situation.

"No, you will do just fine. Some of it can get kind of rough, I admit, but you have to look at it in the same way you look at military training. You'll come out a better man for it."

"I'm sure I will," Turner agrees, his voice sounding less than convinced.

"Well, good luck," I say, shifting around to reach for a folder on the credenza behind me. "I know you will do well. Make an appointment to see me when you finish the course." I have forgotten about Turner already as I begin reading a memo from the Chairman.

"I certainly will, and thanks for your support," Turner says.

I look up, and for a moment or two I can't remember why this young man is standing in front of my desk. Then it comes to me — a candidate for Room 111.

"Certainly, certainly. Don't mention it," I say, turning back to the memo as Turner walks through the door.

One thing remains before I head for the executive garage. I reach for the telephone.

"Hello." Dr. Mirsch's voice has already become a little unfamiliar to me.

"Yes?"

"Listen, cancel my appointment for tonight, will you? Something's come up, and I won't be able to make it."

"Would you like me to schedule you at another time?"

"Let me get back to you on that, will you?"

"Certainly."

I hang up, pick up my briefcase, and head down the corridor past the guards.

"Good night, sir," one of them says with a respectful smile. "Have a good evening."

I nod and step into the elevator, feeling very pleased with myself for having one of the top jobs in the best company in the world.

ABOUT THE AUTHOR

George Lee Walker has been a speechwriter for Lee Iacocca, at Ford; for the president and the chairman of the board of American Motors; for Governors George Romney and William Milliken of Michigan; and, briefly, for President Gerald Ford. He has also been a journalist and was part of a Pulitzer Prize–winning team at the *Detroit Free Press*. *The Chronicles of Doodah* is his first novel.